Instant People-Reading Through Handwriting

Anne Conway

NEWCASTLE PUBLISHING CO., INC.
North Hollywood, California
1991

Library of Congress Cataloging-in-Publication Data

Conway, Anne.
    [How to know everything about anyone through handwriting]
    Instant people reading through handwriting / Anne Conway.
      p. cm.
    Originally published: How to know everything about anyone through
handwriting. c1987.
    Includes index.
    ISBN 0-8069-6854-0
    1. Graphology. I. Title.
BF891.C66   1989
155.2'82—dc19   88-27114
                                       CIP

To the Reader:

    The author and editor of this manual have taken painstaking efforts to maintain the anonymity and rights of privacy of all persons whose handwriting samples appear herein. With respect to the handwriting samples of any person who is not a public figure, such samples may in fact have been altered, for purposes of concealing their identity, and will not necessarily be actual examples of any person's true penmanship. Notwithstanding this, if it occurs that any person is thought to be identified, on the basis of any handwriting sample contained herein, the reader should bear in mind that the text accompanying each respective sample represents only the authors' analysis of said sample, based on generally-accepted graphological principles, and makes no comment on the character of any real person.

First published in paperback in 1989 by Sterling Publishing Co., Inc.
Two Park Avenue, New York, N.Y. 10016
Originally published in hardcover under the
title, "How To Know Everything about
Anyone Through Handwriting," © 1987
by Anne Conway

FIRST EDITION
A NEWCASTLE BOOK
First printing
10 9 8 7 6 5 4 3 2 1
Printed in the United States of America

DEDICATION

For my affectionate, inspiring Thinker husband, Jim, who wanted me to share the methods I used to get us together, and how we're making it happily and ever after. This is also for my mom, Lucille Silver, who taught me how to teach—with love, caring and realism. And for little Aimee.

ACKNOWLEDGEMENTS

Thank you to Al Saunders, my courageous publisher who sees the possibilities and future of this book. Thank you to Sheila Barry, my brilliant editor who recognized this book in the first place, pruned it and spiffed it up. Thanks to Maggie Saylor and Evelyn Budd Michaels—my excellent teachers. Thanks to Sheila Lowe for bringing together the Los Angeles County Chapter of American Handwriting Analysis Foundation and for her invaluable second opinions. Thanks to Dena Sible of Chicago and Nadelle Claypool of Denver— two brilliant graphologists who support me in my work. Thanks to Vi Rogers, editor of the National Singles Register, who has given my column a nice home over the years. Thanks to Edward Di Esso, my best friend, finest editor and favorite writer who ignites my creativity. To my family—Robert and Melen Silver, the Hesses and MacDonoughs. And to the late Roger (Droodles) Price for his devoted friendship, praise and encouragement.

Contents

Part 4—You in Relationships

Part 5—The Letters—A to Z

1. Handwriting: Your Guide to Yourself

Handwriting unveils the mysteries of the soul. You can actually find out why you're here, what lessons you should be learning and if you're doing a good job learning those lessons. In that sense, your handwriting is like a report card. You can tell just about anything you want to know about a person from the symbols in handwriting. If you compare handwritings, you can even determine the compatibility of the people who wrote them.

Your handwriting reveals how passionately you kiss, which traffic lane you drive in, what kind of greeting cards you send, how you behave in long grocery store lines and how often you call your mother. In a more practical vein, your handwriting can pinpoint perfect career choices, creative potential, self-imposed hurdles, irritating habits and lovable qualities.

This book is different from other handwriting analysis books in two ways. First this book will shake up every idea about handwriting that you've ever had. After you read it, you'll never look at a page of script in the same way again. Second, while others say they won't pigeonhole you, this book will. It will label you, and you'll love it as if "Adolfo" was on your backside pocket. This book will give your handwriting a designer name and a place in the sun, a "sign" of its own, actually.

I'll tell you stories that give you an entirely new way of looking at yourself and everyone you know, and by the last page, you'll be able to assess the potential of any relationship. Don't tell my husband, but I wouldn't have dated him if I hadn't seen his handwriting first.

There are plenty of other advantages in learning handwriting analysis, too. For one thing, you can stop feeling guilty for not loving those family members who are so easy to loathe. You know who I mean, that Goody Two Shoes sister, for example, who has made you look bad for twenty years. You're the only one who knows she cheated at Mr. Potato Head and Cootie, and she'd cheat again tomorrow if you gave her half a chance. So when you get to the Red Light chapter, dig up that letter she wrote from the Peace Corps, and you'll see huge capitals, high t-bars and tall, loopy letters. Aha! You were right: pathological liar. She can't see herself for who she is, poor thing, but you don't have to beat up on yourself for wanting her to change.

Two warnings: You won't ever find the perfect handwriting. After all, you won't find the perfect mate either. Don't worry though. If you're like most people, you too might leave a mere scrape of Rocky Road at the bottom of a carton.

Second warning: Don't analyze your parents' handwriting. It's too difficult to be objective about them. You'll look at their handwriting and forget everything in this book.

When I lecture, I'm almost always asked the following questions. You probably want them answered, too.

QUESTIONS AND ANSWERS

Q: My handwriting changes all the time. Does that mean I have a split personality? Can it still be analyzed?

A: That's not uncommon. Maybe. And yes. It can all be analyzed. Elements of handwriting change because we have different moods, we react differently to new situations. These changes are reflected in writing size, upper case letter sizes, slant and spacing between words and lines. However, basic letter formations, margins and signatures remain relatively stable.

Q: Can you analyze printing?

A: Some aspects of personality such as confidence, generosity and communication styles may be deduced from printing. But handwriting analysis as we know it, graphology, is based mostly on upstrokes, while printed letters are formed by downstrokes. Chronic printers may be saying subconsciously that they prefer to have an ambiguous image. Architects and draftsmen print for legibility's sake on blueprints, and they may continue to print off the job from habit.

Q: Can you tell if I fake my handwriting?

A: You might be able to fake a couple of lines, but you won't be able to keep it up.

Q: Is handwriting analysis a psychic science?

A: No. And it's unrelated to astrology, numerology, ESP or any form of metaphysics. Recently the Dewey Decimal System moved handwriting analysis from *Occult* to *Psychology* (much to the chagrin of the psychology establishment). So if you want to read more books on handwriting, go to the psychology section.

Q: Can French or German writing be analyzed?

A: Yes, if any handwriting uses the alphabet and travels from left to right across the page, you'll be able to analyze it. But it's important for you to have a sample of the writing style the person was originally taught. For instance, French people use a capital "J" instead of the capital "I." That makes a big difference because the personal pronoun "I" is the most important individual letter to be analyzed.

Q: Is graphology scientific?

A: Yes, but it's a science that depends on the talent of the graphologist. In that way it's like clinical psychology. And because no psychological test works 100 percent of the time, graphology prides itself as coming in at 94 percent accurate. If you'd like to look up scientific and psychological journal articles, look under *Graphology*. There are literally hundreds that verify graphological reliability.

Q: Is it true that graphology is used in Europe for personnel selection?

A: Yes. In France, for instance, handwriting analysis is often given the same respect as empirically based psychological testing and evaluation. Eighty percent of European corporations use it for the purpose of hiring the best person for the job.* But that doesn't go on only in Europe. You may be surprised to know General Electric, International Harvester, U.S. Steel, Firestone Tire Company and over 3,000 other United States companies have used graphology for personnel selection.

*Wall Street Journal, September 3, 1985, front page.

Q: Is graphology difficult to learn?

A: I don't think so. I've been teaching it for six years and my students seem to find the course easy, fun and useful. But it's up to you to practice. Like learning to throw pottery on a wheel, play tennis and train a puppy, it takes patience and practice.

Q: How soon will I be able to analyze handwriting?

A: Today. And as soon as you start practicing. But a word of caution: As a beginner, you need to develop objectivity; don't jump to conclusions based on a few written words. Do not analyze unless you have a whole page of handwriting on unlined paper. Without that, your results will not be accurate, and you may get frustrated when people tell you you're wrong. And it's demeaning to graphology as a science to treat it lightly.

So—when you meet someone who has what you consider to be perfect handwriting, and bells start ringing in your head, stop a moment and think. It's very easy for a beginning graphologist to get all excited about one aspect of handwriting and overlook others completely, coming up with an entirely misleading analysis. For instance, you may discover a sense of humor stroke and ignore the down-slanted and pointed t-bars. What you will neglect to put together is that the sense of humor is aimed sarcastically at other people.

In a new friendship you may become entranced with the possibilities, assuming that your acquaintance is going to be the best friend you've ever had. And as a result, you'll downplay any negative indications in the handwriting. There is no perfect friend, mate or parent. We all need to develop objectivity and patience.

Q: Where do I start?

A: At the beginning. Where else?

Part 1
The Basic
Personality: Slant

WHAT'S YOUR SLANT?

The first thing to do to evaluate your own handwriting is to get a ball point pen and a sheet of 8 1/2" x 11" unlined paper. Fill the sheet with your natural handwriting. Don't copy from an encyclopedia. Express yourself in a few spontaneous paragraphs. It doesn't matter what you write, as long as you do it spontaneously.

Once you have a whole page of writing, look at all the squiggles, shapes and margins. It all reflects who you are, how you live and how you relate to the world around you. You actually developed more than 600 variations from the writing method you were originally taught. A lot of individuality went into developing that unique style of yours that began with your third grade teacher's penmanship poster! If you ever doubted your creativity, you can put that idea to rest!

As you wrote, you began each line at the left and continued writing to the right until you began a new line. Have you ever thought about what it means to write from left to right? Wonder no longer: the left side of the page represents the past, the self, or where you've been. The right side of the page symbolizes the future and other people. It makes sense, because the future is where you're headed when you begin each new line.

Right now we're interested in how you moved your pen up and down as you wrote your way across the page. That's *slant*, and it reflects your underlying, inner emotional responsive nature. This chapter will help you determine which slant type you are, and see how your inner reactions affect the rest of your personality. Slant reveals how you react to all the people and events in your life—from your inside out.

Slant ranges from extreme left to extreme right. Generally speaking, leftward slants signify emotional caution while rightward slants indicate unrestrained enthusiasm.

The more letters lean to the right, the more future-oriented, aggressive, courageous, expressive and reactive the writers are. The farther writing leans to the left, the more passive, past-oriented, covertly defiant, introverted, repressed and cautious the writers are. Vertical writing shows independence, self-reliance, emotional control and a balance between extro- and introversion. The slant scale ranges from left to right, from detached to attached and from independent to dependent.

I call the backward slanter the "Mender," the vertical writer the "Thinker," and right slanters the "Juggler," "Pleaser" and "Reactor." The one who slants every which way, I call the "Chameleon."

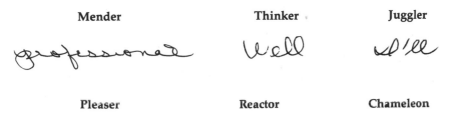

Mender	Thinker	Juggler

Pleaser	Reactor	Chameleon

To measure slant, you need to calculate the angle of the upstrokes, the strokes that rise from the baseline. To help you determine the average degree of the slant, use the gauge below. It may be more convenient to pick up a protractor at the stationery store and mark the degree lines on it to match this diagram:

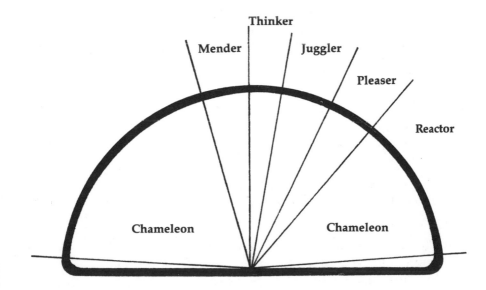

First, look at the "l's." Notice how the measuring line rises from the baseline and travels straight through the top of the letter.

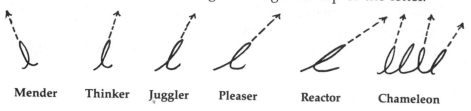

| Mender | Thinker | Juggler | Pleaser | Reactor | Chameleon |

To determine slant, you'll require at least 50 measurements. It's good to use "l's" for this purpose, but you can also measure "b" and "h" upper loops. Draw in the slant lines, as shown above in a different color ink than the one you used in your sample. Start where the letters *begin to rise* from the baseline and extend your slant line to exactly the point at which the stroke begins to *come down*. Place the horizontal line of the protractor over the written baseline and find the number on the curved arc. In this sample, for example, the angle of the first "l" is 105, the second is 80.

Begins to rise at arrow   **Begins to come down at arrow**   **Measuring line**

Add the 50 measurements. Divide by 50. You now have the average slant degree.

THINKER	= 81-90 degrees
JUGGLER	= 65-80 degrees
PLEASER	= 50-64 degrees
REACTOR	= 5-49 degrees
MENDER	= 91-105 degrees (to the left)
CHAMELEON	= 5-105 degrees

It's tempting to get lazy and simply eyeball or guess the slant. But you could be wrong. Not all writing is as it appears. For instance, Chameleon writing can fool you because it often looks like

Thinker writing: straight up and down. Some Thinker writing, when you measure it, turns out to be Juggler. If your calculation places the average slant on a borderline between two slants, read the slant descriptions for both sides. If you arrive at 65 degrees as your average slant, for example, the writing will be a combination of Juggler and Pleaser. It must be right on the border to be combination of both slants, because there are not that many degrees within each slant. If after reading the slant description, you don't feel that it's correct, measure your handwriting when you're in another mood. Your slant will change during the day and according to your moods.

Each slanter personality has its own basic attitudes toward life—its own ways of thinking and feeling, taking action, falling in love and helping others. Let's take a look at them.

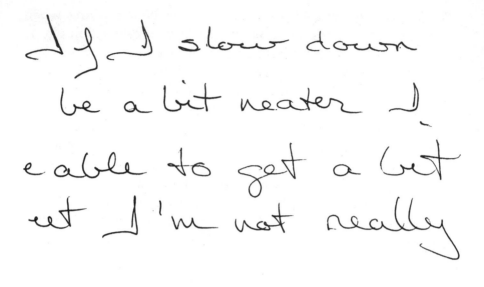

2. The Thinker

On independence: I can do it myself.
On thinking and feeling: I think, therefore I am.
On taking action: I look before crawling.
On helping others: How can I help you?
On love: I love you now that I know you.

The best thing about Thinkers is also their potential downfall. They're extraordinarily sweet. That can be extraordinarily frustrating to their friends. What's so exasperating about being sweet? It's that they're sweet to absolutely everybody—even to their enemies— especially to their enemies. And because they're so "nice," they don't stand up for themselves.

Thinkers want peace at any cost. And they won't usually challenge incompetent people. You'll seldom find them arguing with car mechanics, wrestling rowdy kids to the ground or battling it out with the bank. Thinkers are modern-day King Solomons, and people look up to them for fair judgments.

Why do Thinkers value peace and harmony over life itself? Well, perhaps they were the self-appointed peace-makers in their original families. Or possibly everyone else in their homes was downright hysterical, and so they carry a Kissinger-like responsibility into all their adult relationships. Every worrier in the neighborhood feels free to drop in and dump problems on Thinkers—especially when they're eating dinner or watching the last episode of *Masterpiece Theater*. But Thinkers love it. They're fulfilling their life's destiny.

Thinkers have emotions, for sure, but seldom will they get passionate about them. They feel more comfortable being aloof and logical. When confronted with someone else's emotional crises, they offer advice, but they don't let anyone ruffle their feathers with such problems. When pushed too hard, (or relentlessly nagged), they simply walk away. It may sometimes seem cruel or uncaring of them, but it isn't. The Thinker's role in life is to provide stability for all those others. You may feel pounding your head against the wall when a Thinker refuses to fight, but you'll soon learn to value those serene ways. After all, if you've been around fighters all your life, it's a real treat to meet Thinkers who will keep cool and love unconditionally—even though you may suspect that they love everyone unconditionally!

Thinkers are shuffling slowpokes when it comes to making decisions and absolute snails when it comes to making changes. All right, you say, most of us are far too impulsive anyway. You can use a Thinker around to slow you down in order to gain a better perspective. After all, where would Captain Kirk be without Mr. Spock? (Mr. Spock is sure to have been a Thinker!)

Thinkers are slow to break out of old routines. They would rather say "yes" to the demands of family and friends than "no," even when they have something they really want to do. It gets to be a habit with them. So it's easy to take advantage of Thinker good nature.

Thinkers also tend to be romantically passive. Is that because they're cautious? Or because they enjoy their independence? In any case, they want all the facts (and, of course, never will have them all). So they aren't likely to be walking dynamos or sweep people off their feet.

Let's suppose you're in love with a Thinker. You're contemplating marriage, but the Thinker is dating other people. What on earth can you do to change that picture? Here's what won't work:

1. Ultimatums won't work:
   YOU: If you don't stop dating all those others, I'll jump out the window.
   THINKER: Happy landing.
2. Commands won't work:
   YOU: I got tickets for the ballet for Saturday night. You'd better break your other date.
   THINKER: I'll see if Pat can go with you.
3. Blackmail won't work either:
   YOU: If you don't set a wedding date, I won't take care of your cat anymore.
   THINKER: No sweat—she ran away last night.

What can you do to speed up Thinker decisions? Nothing. Being involved with them means taking responsibility for your own life. If you want to be with them, all you can do is wait until they decide you're the one for them. And when they do decide on you, you probably won't ever have to doubt their love again.

Once you've captured the heart of a Thinker, you're in for a relationship unlike any other you've had before. Thinkers are not going to fight you. (That can be infuriating.) And they're not going to tell you when they're angry with you. You might get that "uh-oh" feeling that you did something wrong, but you won't be able to drag out of them what you did. Or they may choose to downplay the whole matter. The reason (besides wanting to keep the peace) may be that they see no useful purpose in challenging something in you that you probably won't change. A Thinker, for example, would never tell his wife he hated her friends. A Thinker wife would never ask her husband to keep his sister out of their house. Doesn't that make sense?

Your Thinker friends are chicken when it comes to returning things to the store for a refund. They'd rather keep the sweater that's two sizes too large than return it. After all, it's embarrassing to confront a manager who might say no. Thinkers don't like to get into situations that are out of their control.

Family life and friendships are everything to Thinker (unless their family is too crazy to be around). They're usually loyal and faithful lovers and maintain friendships from nursery to grave. Harmonizing with them is easy if you allow them to be nice, loyal and indecisive. Their greatest problem is with other people trying to change them.

One final note. Some Thinkers may not fit some parts of the descriptions given here—especially the ones about being sane and logical and appearing calm and collected. When you find a Thinker who is very emotional, look at other handwriting traits. You'll probably see overly large and expansive writing. And you'll probably notice complicated a's and o's. This means your Thinker friends are out of touch with their feelings. If they don't identify feelings, they store them. And when they stockpile enough unexpressed feelings, they're going to be in emotional trouble.

Most people write in "Thinkese" now and then. Actually, nine out of ten people say they write differently at different times, and what they mean is that they write with a Juggler slant most of the time, and then shift into Thinker writing. Thinker writing appears out of nowhere on grocery lists, memos and thank you letters. What does it mean? We tend to write in Thinkese when our emotions aren't involved, when we're in an objective state of mind.

You as a Thinker

Being a Thinker you already know that some of your biggest problems arise from other people trying to change you. They urge you to spend less time on the phone listening to all your friends' problems. Your secretary threatens to quit if you don't let her organize your desk. And your family begs you to toss out that fringed leather vest from 1968 and the exercise machines and all that other junk, because if people ever tried to find anything in your closet, they might get seriously injured.

So, if your habits don't bother you, install a separate phone line for yourself, hire a sloppy secretary and lock your closet door. Assert yourself by conveying in no uncertain terms that you like your life exactly as is. Or, and it may be easier for you, compromise a little.

The Thinker Mate

The way to reach Thinker wives and husbands is almost always through their appetites. All varieties of appetites. They love to eat, entertain, redecorate their homes and massage each other.

If your Thinkers are sloppy packrats, and it's driving you up the wall, you can always throw out their stuff when they're not home. No one knows why, but every Thinker man has weights he has never pressed, except from the Christmas tree to the garage. And probably every Thinker woman would rather wear baggy jeans and sweat socks than dresses and nylons.

They're not likely to change old habits, so you'll probably just have to learn to live with them. But if your biggest complaint is their resistance to change, it's time to look at the bright side. Thinkers may be the best mates because they're loving, emotionally supportive, slow to anger and they usually adore their children. If you hear people brag that their spouses are saints, chances are that those mates are Thinkers.

The Thinker Child

Thinker children need to be trusted to make their own decisions. You can't force them into anything anyway. You already know they'll only clean their rooms when they want to. They'll only quit torturing their siblings when they're bored with it. And they'll only behave when it seems logical to them. The major goal of Thinker children is to outwit authority figures. They also seem to be impervious to guilt. So how do you discipline a Thinker child? You don't. They eventually learn to discipline themselves. All you can do is praise the good things they do while trying to overlook the bad.

The Thinker Boss

Thinker bosses are highly unlikely to be critical of your work, at least openly. They'd rather find you another job than fire you. They tend to think of you as a co-worker rather than an underling. Don't be afraid to ask for time off, two hour lunches and occasional weekends for ski trips. They'll understand.

The Thinker Employee

Your Thinker employees will be your friends, too. You may want to clean their desks for them once a month, but you may never be forgiven for doing that without their permission. Perhaps their best qualities are dependability, emotional stability, love of team spirit and the ability to produce under pressure. Doesn't that sound like the ideal employee?

The Thinker Friend

There are few greater pleasures in life than having Thinker friends. You get almost all the Thinker goodies with none of the frustrations. The only serious trap is that they would rather end your friendship than confront you with something you did to offend them.

The Thinker In-Law

Thinker in-laws will believe you can do no wrong. You'll never be criticized or taken for granted. And they'll always be willing to babysit. If you get a feeling that they don't like you, it may be very difficult to find out what you did to offend them. They don't want to confront you. It's probably best to ask your spouse to intervene.

I also want to let that I'm glad I've gotten opportunity to get to side of "wonderful cha- group. In whatever he really didn't get a ch

3. The Juggler

On independence: I can do it myself, with your support.
On thinking and feeling: I think, therefore I don't often feel.
On taking action: I leap while looking.
On helping others: I'll help you if I have time.
On love: I'll love you if you're worth it.

Circus jugglers mesmerize audiences. They assume striking poses as they keep plates, torches or swords moving simultaneously in midair, and their rhythm is mysterious and fascinating. If you've never tried to juggle, you won't understand the difficulty. It looks so easy. Ha!

Jugglers are the most emotionally complicated of all slant types. They give the impression they have life arranged in order and can handle any crisis with the greatest of ease. Some can. Others fake it.

If Jugglers have gotten their lives ship-shape, they're able to relate to anyone with what seems like psychic ability. Everyone feels understood by them and is.

But the Jugglers who fake it may not even know themselves that their control is merely a facade. When their guard is down, it's clear that they're bundles of self-doubt, easily defeated and obsessed over petty details. That's when you begin to reverse your first impression that a Juggler is a sane, rational creature.

How can there be such discrepancy within the same slant? It's because Jugglers are half Thinker and half Pleaser. They strive to be objective and in touch with their feelings simultaneously, and that's practically impossible.

Jugglers want to be sane and rational in love, like Thinkers, but they are highly emotionally charged. Even though Jugglers would prefer to rely on rational ways to experience emotions, they need to learn to trust their feelings.

Jugglers experience dreadful inner conflict when their emotions don't cooperate with their intellects. For example, if Jugglers break up with a lover, they decide that the relationship didn't really matter anyway. And so they run to the nearest distraction. But their inner sense of loss eventually catches up with them, because feelings don't go away. They get moody and irritable because they're playing games with themselves.

Jugglers definitely need to create a place in their lives for passion, even though they mistrust it. They prefer to manufacture a cool, Thinkerish image, but they're emotional and must admit it.

It may sound paradoxical, but Jugglers approach their emotions through thinking first, feeling later. Thoughts and fantasies stimulate their emotional reactions. Jugglers may consider their feelings second-rate thoughts that shouldn't be taken into consideration. But then they'll turn around and make impulsive romantic decisions as though their rational judgments don't matter.

Jugglers appear to be Thinkers because they enjoy the "nice guy" image, but Jugglers don't feel they have to be that way all the time the way Thinkers do. They can transform themselves into tough guys when necessary, even though they'd rather avoid confrontations, too.

Jugglers also want to be loyal, but not at any cost. When they see what they think are greener pastures, they often jump the fence—abandoning relationships, jobs and "hangouts." They can be opportunistic in a flash. They may regret their decisions later and feel guilty, but that won't stop them.

Like Thinkers, Jugglers may have been self-appointed family peacemakers, but they only accepted that role grudgingly. They may listen to everyone's problems and feel compelled to patch up other people's lives, but that doesn't mean they won't feel imposed upon.

Jugglers strive for objectivity as Thinkers do, but then suddenly they act irrationally and make decisions based only on their immediate feelings. This comes from their Pleaser half. So they vacillate between being brutal, sane and rational on the one hand, and making unexpected, mad, whirlwind decisions on the other.

When they manage to stifle their self-doubts and explore their talents, expressing the creative, artistic side of their nature, Jugglers are usually rewarded. But when they base their careers solely on making money, they aren't as likely to be successful.

In romance, Jugglers may fake passion, but they don't really want to, and they feel uncomfortable doing it. They say all the right words, but if they're not as intensely involved as they pretend, they don't feel good about it. So in relationships they may flirt and run. And the seductees never know what hit them, because it's difficult to know when a Juggler is being genuine.

Once truly in love, Jugglers display a passion that surprises even themselves. They suspect they aren't capable of deep feelings, but that's not true. Once they've found the right person, their love can last a lifetime. Then they learn to trust and enjoy all those intense feelings they've spent years avoiding.

Some other types, Pleasers, for example, need to be involved in relationships in order to feel like a whole person. Sometimes Jugglers do, too. They require a home base and support from one important person in their lives. But in order to create a love focus, they must be ready to settle down. Because of this, their relationships are likely to become more stable when the Jugglers are in their thirties and tired of running around.

Many Jugglers believe career comes first, and often female Jugglers have difficulties deciding between a career and a family. But when they find a person who understands and loves them, they make room for both quite easily. They know how to juggle!

If they don't find the right person, they easily lose themselves in their careers. And they may convince themselves their emotional life doesn't count very much.

In long-term relationships many Jugglers fall into nonfeeling states. Then their lovers wonder what they did to make the passion disappear. It isn't anything they did; it's that Jugglers easily get preoccupied. Sure of their love life, they may often take their lovers for granted. Then a shake-up may be needed to make them focus on the relationship again.

When troubled or confused, Jugglers are not likely to ask their mates for advice—especially when the confusion *concerns* their mates. For example, many Jugglers get upset when their mates seem too busy for them. They take it personally and feel rejected. So they consult with friends. When these "secret" conversations take place, their mates may feel alienated and not know why. It's important for Jugglers to stuff their pride and talk about the problem with their mates: "What can I do to help so we can spend more time together?" When they take the direct approach, they usually get what they want.

You as a Juggler

Being unsure of your intellectual capabilities, you place tremendous importance on cleverness. You value being sane and rational, but you seldom feel that you have achieved that state of mind.

Diplomas and academic awards may give you secure feelings, but you never quite believe that you earned them. The fact of the matter is that deep down, you'd much rather be rewarded for a heartfelt, humanitarian act.

To feel more confident in your daily life, stop and give yourself credit for the growth you gain through experience. Eventually you will realize that only through experience will you get the knowledge you want.

So it is experience more than intellect that makes you as a Juggler satisfied and at peace with yourself. But as a Juggler, you also need to stay in touch with your feelings. If you don't, you may find yourself suffering from mysterious depressions. It won't help to cover up your emotions by being glib. Probably one or both of your parents were negative or judgmental. As a result, you're prone to black-and-white thinking, classifying everything as all good or all bad. Let go of the rating system, if you can, and learn to evaluate life events in shades of grey.

The Juggler Mate

If your Juggler mate feels understood, you will feel appreciated more than you've ever felt in your life. Jugglers can be the most demonstrative and supportive of mates. So realize that you need to acknowledge their feelings, make it very clear that you do, and you will truly win the Juggler's affections forever. When they complain, try to see their point. You don't have to agree, but do make an attempt to understand their point of view. They also need you to take the lead in arranging outings, weekend trips and vacations, because they're prone to workaholism. Jugglers may moan and groan on the way to Cozumel, but they'll have a great time once they're away from their desks.

The Juggler Child

Juggler children are seldom bored. They keep busy and, generally, out of trouble. It's unlikely they'll ever steal a car or throw rocks through windows. Because they're so concerned getting your approval, they won't be very sneaky or rebellious. But that doesn't mean a parent's relationship with a Juggler child will be trouble-free.

Juggler children tend to adopt a parental role when they become too aware of their parents' problems. They act like little adults and miss out on much of the fun of childhood. Their independence and intelligence can sometimes encourage their parents to talk with them as they would to a friend or counselor. And little Jugglers will take those problems too seriously. That doesn't mean you have to hide your feelings from them, patronize them or be dishonest. It just means you need a special awareness so that you don't dwell on difficulties to the point where the children feel your problems are their own.

The Juggler Boss

Juggler bosses will probably be more critical than you thought they'd be before you went to work for them. After all, they live to work and believe everyone else should, too. It may be difficult for you to see any vulnerability in them. It is also difficult to have a friendship with Juggler bosses, because they feel they lose authority if they get friendly. So respect any distance they require, work hard and you'll have a good working relationship.

The Juggler Employee

Juggler employees work best with other Jugglers, but they can work well with any slant type. They especially like having Thinkers around, because Thinkers are as work-oriented as they are. As an employer, you probably won't have to motivate your Juggler employees to work hard. In fact, you may have force them to take a vacation.

Jugglers usually don't need supervision, provided you tell them exactly what you expect of them. They need definite job descriptions. As long as they aren't stuck with covering up for other employees' mistakes, they should work out fine for you.

The Juggler Friend

Jugglers put friends on the back burner when they have too much work and too little time, which is almost always. So when you don't hear from Juggler friends for a couple of months, give them a call. Something is undoubtedly keeping them busy, and it's probably interesting. Be prepared to make the first move. Jugglers can't help getting preoccupied. If you take their lack of attention personally, you're missing the point that work comes first in their lives.

The Juggler In-Law

You won't be able to hide a thing from Juggler in-laws. When you and your spouse fight, they'll know it psychically. They may know you're expecting a baby before you know. Their most charming quality is that they'll trust you and your mate to solve your own problems. They're the least likely in-laws to pry into your affairs. They're just too busy.

If you need some assist finding alternative medi surance, you are welco contact the representative enclosed card.

4. The Pleaser

On independence: We'll do it together, won't we?
On thinking and feeling: I feel, therefore I'm in love.
On taking action: I leap before looking.
On helping others: Let me do that for you.
On love: I'll love you forever.

Pleasers respond to life as children to Disneyland—spontaneously and with abandon. Some of the rides might scare them while others tickle their fancy, but they respond wholeheartedly to each attraction.

Pleasers are the first ones we have talked about that depend upon being involved in a relationship. Thinkers and Jugglers don't have to be one half of a couple in order to feel good about themselves, but Pleasers do. (Reactors are even more dependent than Pleasers, but more about them later.)

There are two kinds of Pleasers. One type reacts from feelings of insecurity, the other from feelings of love. The first type responds to others out of a sense of obligation and guilt, while the second "heart-centered" type is genuinely giving.

Insecure Pleasers try to influence the thoughts and behavior of others indirectly. They often manipulate people in order to get their way. They are also great martyrs. They actually seem to enjoy playing the victim role and having others feel sorry for them. And since Pleasers are passionately emotional, the people closest to them are required to take the Pleaser side in all arguments—even the ones they're involved in themselves. It's hard to win with a Pleaser. They can stay on one point for months! And once they hate somebody, they won't easily forgive or forget (especially if they write with deep pressure).

Heart-centered Pleasers are deeply concerned with being loved, and they live to express themselves. Sociable, friendly and outgoing, they're also the first type discussed so far that are outright (and sometimes extravagant) extroverts.

Pleaser enthusiasm is contagious and difficult to resist. They believe they can't do enough for the ones they love and are likely to feel guilty if they suspect they could have done more.

One Pleaser I know remembered her best friend's birthday was the next day. She alerted all their mutual friends and her friend's family. She baked a double-decker cake, cleaned and decorated her friend's apartment and wrapped a few gifts within 24 hours. When the birthday boy marvelled at this Pleaser's resourcefulness, she didn't understand what he was talking about. Caring and getting things done at short notice is second nature to her.

Pleasers are often impulse buyers. Not all are extravagant, but they are apt to spend money without considering their budgets, especially if they leave large spaces between letters and words. If letters and words are tightly spaced, they will be more cautious with money, energy and emotions. The looser the writing, the more extroverted and extravagant Pleaser will be.

Future-oriented, Pleasers like to plan ahead. But once they formulate a plan, they want immediate action and instant results. They become impatient when they have to wait. They also like changes in their home environment. Living with a Pleaser means never knowing where furniture will be when you get home.

Pleasers are impulsive and likely to enter into relationships without considering the pitfalls. They will be convinced they can make an alcoholic stop drinking and a kleptomaniac stop stealing—simply because they love them. Pleasers believe that solely on the power of their love, their loved ones will be freed from all undesirable traits. Of course, what Pleasers may find undesirable in their lovers' personalities may not bother the lover one bit. And when the lover doesn't change, nudging may turn into nagging.

Many Pleasers are compulsive matchmakers because they can't bear seeing their friends alone or lonely. Because they're so dependent on relationships, they think everyone else is too. Often they're successful at their matchmaking, but the danger for them is that they may be left behind. When things do work out, their friends may want a little privacy. Because Pleasers want things to be perfect, they're apt get involved in things that aren't their business, and then get hurt when they're not quite welcomed.

A very sunny side to Pleaser personalities is their charitable outlook, a liking for helping those who can't help themselves. Pleasers are deeply affected by the suffering of others. As a result, many Pleaser careers center on caring for others. They are often happiest as nurses, teachers, workers with the handicapped, secretaries, psychotherapists, and yes, even graphologists.

Unlike Thinkers, Pleasers are passionate shoppers and they also return their purchases with a vengeance. Shopping may become a hobby, and it is often essential to Pleasers' self-esteem to get fantastic bargains. If Pleasers aren't satisfied with the merchandise, they won't be afraid of anybody—let alone a store manager. Coming from a long line of choosy shoppers, my Pleaser mother takes anything and everything back to the store—from bananas to empty tortilla chip bags. The store managers all know her and love her, because she also offers them ingenious suggestions for improving their merchandising.

It doesn't take much for Pleaser to get deeply involved academically with almost any course they choose. Often, when they take electives at college, they change majors. A single Pleaser transcript generally looks as if the course loads of two or three very different individuals got jumbled up in the computer!

Pleasers are likely to have more than one career during their lifetimes. Prone to depression if their hearts aren't in their work, they often change careers midway through life. They dread retirement and aren't usually happy doing nothing.

You as a Pleaser

You act out a very strange contradiction. You're the most courageous of the slant types, and yet, you don't know that you are. If you asked your friends, they'd probably all tell you that they *admire* you for your courage.

What you actually need is more confidence in yourself. Of course, you're fearful when you put your best work forward to be judged and you're anxious about how it will be received. Everyone is. Your true courage comes out when you face real danger and emergencies that require your skills and knowledge. Have no doubt that you possess that kind of bravery.

Whether it's on the surface or buried deeply, inside you is the fear that you aren't good enough. You depend on praise from others and discount your own judgment.

But remember there are two kinds of Pleasers. One reacts out of fear and gets stomachaches under stressful circumstances. The other Pleaser acts out of love and what they do comes from the heart.

If you're the fearful, gut-reacting Pleaser, it may help to expect less from other people. You probably realized by now that the more gratitude you expect, the less you get. So when you give, ask yourself how many strings you attach to your presents. Then try to snip them off.

All Pleasers fantasize about what they should have said after it's too late. If you expect you can learn to think faster on your feet, forget it. You're always going to be taking the other person's feelings into account, so you're not going to be likely to be able to come up with the glib retorts Jugglers and Thinkers seem to have at their tonguetips.

If you want to feel greater inner peace, you'll need to develop objectivity. You want to see the good in everyone, and you think everyone cares as deeply as you do. You're apt to be disappointed when these expectations are not met. If you become more realistic, however, you'll be happier with friends, family and yourself.

The Pleaser Mate

It's not necessary to cater to *all* those moods and agree with every Pleaser opinion, but to keep comfortable with you, and to feel love in return, Pleasers need to feel understood. All you need to say is, "I know you hate it, darling, when I talk on the phone all evening, but I need to keep up with my friends." (Don't forget to say "darling.") You can often win a Pleaser over simply by acknowledging those negative feelings.

The Pleaser Child

What adorable, loving, kind human beings! They'd never do anything wrong! Do you know why? They're too busy spying and gathering evidence on Thinker children. And they're not above tattling. They think it makes them look better.

The major goal of a Pleaser child is to be popular—more popular then anyone has ever been. Pleaser kids want friends more than A's on their report cards. And since these junior public relations experts probably have more friends than spaces in their addresss books, they won't hit the books or plan on a career until they absolutely must.

When Pleasers get their drivers' licenses, they will never drive over 55 mph when an adult is in the car, which may make you wonder why they get so many speeding tickets. The problem is that these Pleasers fear punishment and lie to protect themselves. It might be a good idea to reward them for honesty. They may be less likely to try to hide things.

The Pleaser Boss

Your Pleaser boss could be either your greatest supporter or your worst enemy, but nothing in between. Just remember Pleasers are suckers for compliments. You don't have to flatter them to the extent that you make everyone else in the office sick, but if you honestly praise their work, family or appearance, they will value you more highly. Do not defy a Pleaser. If you're defiant, go to work for a Mender.

The Pleaser Employee

If the Pleasers you work with aren't overburdened, and if you treat them right, you have instant supporters for your projects. Handle them as you would a Pleaser boss, and they will probably work nights and weekends or, anyway, help you all they can. Just don't ever, ever, ever suggest that your Pleaser employee lose weight or stop smoking. If you do, you may experience a cold war.

The Pleaser Friend

Pleaser friends must be appreciated. If you really want to stay on their good side, give gifts that equal the value of the ones they give you—if you can afford it. If you can't, write them poetry.

The Pleaser In-Law

Pleaser in-laws will adore you as long as your mate does. Be careful not to discuss religion or politics with them, though, if their views oppose yours. Arguing usually puts them off, so it's wise to find someone else to banter with.

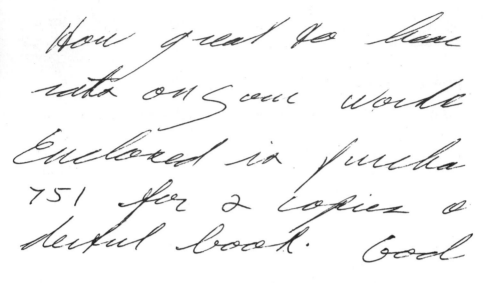

5. The Reactor

On independence: I'll do it alone if you help me.
On thinking and feeling: I let my feelings guide my thinking, and I feel emphatically, therefore I'm passionate.
On taking action: I leap and never look.
On helping others: I am always helping you, you ingrate.
On love: I'd die without you.

Did you ever tell a store clerk you got engaged, only to have her react with such insane joy, you thought she was severely disturbed? You met a Reactor in living color. Reactors are extraordinarily emotional.

Reactor smiles could light darkened football fields and their frowns could make onions cry. They respond so intensely to life that most people think they're exaggerating or faking their excitement. If you try to tease Reactors for getting so excited, they won't understand what the joke is all about. Their enthusiasm is genuine and they will expect you to join them, not stand along the wall poking fun.

Reactors identify so strongly with those around them that they can't separate the problems of others from their own. If, for instance, a Reactor's child punches the kid down the block, she may act as if World War III has begun and create a permanent rift between the two families. Reactors are not about to let their kids settle their own problems.

Reactors are so responsive, they anticipate your needs even before you realize you have any. They're walking solutions in search of a problem. If you don't have a problem, you soon will. Reactors will find some. If that doesn't work, Reactors don't feel needed and are apt to drift away.

When they have a negative outlook, Reactors see potential danger everywhere. You can hear them on the playground: "Don't drink from that fountain, there are germs on it"; in the grocery store: "Don't buy food from a bin, you don't know who touched those rolled oats"; in fiction: "The sky is falling!" Chicken Little was a full-feathered Reactor.

Reactors use enormous amounts of energy just to exist. Experiencing life so intensely, they wear themselves out quite fast. Reactors swing like pendulums out of control from the pits to the peaks but seldom pause in between. Life is never dull with them around.

Reactors are the most dependent and doting of all slant types. Because they appear insecure and seem to need so much attention, you might think they'd demand more than you want to give. But this isn't necessarily true. Reactors can be the most devoted and fun-loving people you'll ever know. Let them wallow in their ever-changing moods, and don't give up on them. Life may seem like a roller coaster sometimes, but what a ride you'll have!

You as a Reactor

You're an absolute cyclone of feelings. And you throw yourself in the middle of anything that excites you, never stopping to evaluate a situation until it's too late. Your passion encompasses people, events and causes. Passion lies at the root of all your motivation.

Your motto is, "If it works great, there's still room for improvement." "Change" is your middle name, because your energy fluctuates constantly and searches for expression. Therefore, your perception of your role in life is to improve the world—to make your mark.

Your energy is also playful. You accept people at face value and like them until they give you a good reason not to. Sometimes your reasons for rejecting people are flimsy, so be careful not to snub those who are actually on your side.

Sometimes you poke your nose where it doesn't belong without realizing your faux pas. Then when you're told to go away, you find it difficult not to take the rejection personally. You see, as a Reactor, you expose people's sensitivities—not out of malice—but out of innocent curiosity.

Now, because Reactors are rare, you probably don't know anyone like yourself. So don't let your Juggler and Thinker friends get you down when they say you're out of bounds. They couldn't possibly understand what it's like to be you.

One last note: As a Reactor you're highly impressionable. You want be believe what other people tell you and don't always bother to check things out for yourself. So it's possible for you to get involved with off-beat religions or cults that aren't really acceptable to you at all, and such impulsive involvements could be dangerous.

The Reactor Mate

It's too late. If you're reading this, you probably already love that Reactor of yours, and you're learning to live with those chaotic moods. You've probably already decided it's worth being on the merry-go-round because of all the love and attention you receive. But when Reactors become unreasonable, don't try to argue the mood away. If you acknowledge the feelings they are going through and subtly direct their attention to something else, it may work to allay their fear. Sometimes, of course, it will drive them up the wall and/or through the roof. Hold on and keep giving love. They'll calm down sooner or later.

The Reactor Child

By the time Reactors are twelve years old, you're going to need to be especially sensitive to their overactive emotions. You can help harness that energy by directing them into esteem-building projects that allow them to be creative and feel good about themselves. If Reactor children are not raised with consistent rewards and punishments and made to feel valued as a family member, they may act out their conflicts as teenagers. For example, if you "ground" your Reactor for two weeks, don't give in and call it off after two days. And if you make promises, keep them. Reactors want so desperately to be good and for you to love them that they quickly feel rejected when they don't get the approval they seek. When that happens, they're susceptible to the lure of drugs and alcohol. And because they react so strongly, they are probably the most prone to addiction.

The Reactor Boss

This employer lives in an entirely emotional world even though it might not seem like it on the surface. Many Reactors try to disguise those tender, vulnerable souls, but whether they do or not, the danger remains that your needs could be ignored. Reactor's deadlines will be *your* deadlines, so expect to stay late, work weekends and carry work home—especially when you'd rather be skiing.

Unless a Reactor really respects your talents, you're not likely to receive the credit you're due. Remember Thinkers are the fair guys, Reactors are not going to be objective. So if you want recognition, appeal to the Reactor's emotions.

The Reactor Employee

Many emotional emergencies will get in the way of work. You may want your own cubicle when Reactor is present in the office in order to get any work done. Reactors love gossip, so be sure anything you say to them in private is okay to say in public.

Getting them to be productive is easy. Give them a workload that would make anyone else want to quit, and they'll thrive. They love a challenge, so when you give them more and more responsibilities, you'll find you won't have to do so much yourself.

The Reactor Friend

These friends aren't going to be the world's best listeners, because they're busy formulating what they're going to say while you're speaking. They're likely to ask questions, wait a millisecond and then continue talking. The relationship may be frustrating, but your Reactor friend is probably the only one who will come get you at 3 a.m. when your car breaks down—and be delighted to do it, too.

The Reactor In-Law

They react in the same way as Pleaser in-laws, but more so. If you fight with your spouse, you will never be *completely* forgiven. But, of course, a Reactor will be a very doting grandparent. This is the guy driving around with an "Ask Me About My Grandchildren" license plate cover.

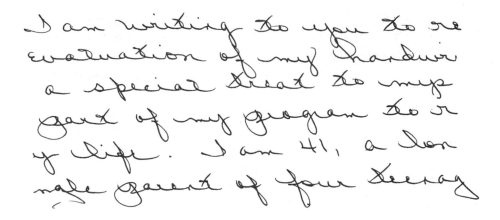

6. The Mender

On independence: I probably didn't do it right. Can you help?
On thinking and feeling: I feel constantly, therefore I'm vulnerable.
On taking action: I leap only when pushed.
On helping others: Are you sure you want *me* to help you?
On love: Love me and I'll adore you.

Whether male or female, Menders tend to their families and enjoy being the caretakers. They volunteer for charity work, take in orphans, stray cats and dogs and foreign exchange students. If you're sick in bed and call your Mender friend, you'll soon have a nice bowl of chicken soup, a back rub and a fluffed pillow. As their handwriting bends to the left, they are known for bending over backwards to make sure everything is Wonderful for you. That's Mender's outer personality.

Their inner core, however, is markedly different from their outer facade. They are "giving" people, but they find it hard (perhaps impossible) to receive the same affection they lavish on others.

To understand Menders, look at their past. That won't be hard to do because they're never emotionally more than two steps away from it. Because their memories are an integral part of their lives, we need to look at the typical Mender biography to understand their personalities.

As children, Menders generally had hard-to-please parents, and as adults, they diligently try to be perfect. They need approval in order to feel okay, but it's difficult to convince them that they are indeed acceptable people. For them to feel good about themselves, they need to realize that attaining perfection is impossible, unrealistic and not really all that desirable.

Often you'll find a very demanding adult in Mender's past who quashed Mender's emotional responsiveness. As a child, for example, the Mender may have been referred to as a crybaby. Whatever the cause, adult Menders come to mistrust their own impulses and stuff their true feelings. That's why they appear reserved. Building their love and trust may take a great deal of patience and a lot of time, but it's worth it. Menders can be some of the most loyal, devoted and adoring friends you'll ever have.

As teenagers, Menders usually feel rejected by their parents, and decide to control their emotions forever more. They figure if they hide behind an uncaring or blank-faced facade, no one will know how they *really* feel inside. Inside is where they feel safe from the domination of other people. But don't waste too much time feeling sorry for them, because Menders can and do take care of themselves very well.

Over the years Menders developed a private rebellion of their own against their past and present misfortunes. And they don't all suffer in silence. Some of them love to relate and relive their problems over and over again. Tactlessly tell them to lighten up, and you won't be welcome company. But if you lend an ear to these woes, you may make a friend for life.

Within five minutes after meeting many Menders, you'll know Everything That Has Ever Gone Wrong in their lives. But something may strike you as strange about that flat tone of voice. Sometimes, when they're telling you about their open heart surgery, they sound as if they're talking about the weather. Emotional expression is missing, and the incongruity may startle you.

As a rule, Menders tiptoe along life's path and try to stay out of trouble. Fearful because they've suffered so much, they wait for the other shoe to drop.

Being timid, Menders won't be extremely passionate or explosive. So if you like to fight, find a Chameleon, a Reactor or a Pleaser.

You might think your Mender acquaintances are snobs until you realize they're merely shy. They're hiding their vulnerability behind a cool, calm facade. A Mender may think, "If people don't see how much I care, they won't know where to aim the arrows when they get mad at me."

My Fair Lady's Professor Higgins is a Mender. (Incidentally, Rex Harrison's real life signature shows a Mender personality, too) He needed to dominate Eliza Doolittle in order to care about her. But throughout the play and movie, he never says, "I love you," nor does he expect her to love him in return. Another Mender trait of Higgins: he can only love someone who needs him (revealing Mender's endearing side). When needed, Mender is powerful.

Before you become involved with Menders, think. They'll be hurt if you impulsively commit yourself to them and then suddenly back out. But keeping a relationship going may cost you social freedom, because Mender may get jealous of your outside friendships. Try getting Menders interested in your other friends, and most of the time you'll find they fit right in.

I used to think Menders were masochistic and incapable of having fun until I looked more closely. I found that when their friends and families stopped burdening them with problems Menders often blossomed into truly creative individuals. When they take that cloak of sorrow off and put it away, there's pure glee in their faces. One carefree day, I thought my Mender sister-in-law was drunk, but she was actually just happy!

You as a Mender

You have a very sweet nature and a desire to make everything bad good. If there weren't anything to fix, you'd feel useless. It's only when you feel that it's your responsibility to intervene and get everyone out of trouble that you suffer.

Perhaps you should ask yourself whether concentrating on everyone else's problems excuses you from solving your own. Whose life are you leading? If you become over involved with the "needs" of family members or co-workers, instead of expressing your creativity through caring for the helpless, you may be avoiding your own destiny.

The Mender Mate

Mender mates bend over backwards to please their families. You'll feel loved, treasured and deeply cared for, but make sure your Mender spouse isn't projecting the image of a rejecting parent onto you. If that happens, be loving, supportive and share your feelings of wanting to be accepted as yourself. Take an active parenting role with your children, or your kids might adopt your spouse's fearfulness.

The Mender Child

Backward slanting children may be telling you something. They are hurting inside and probably feeling rejected by you or your spouse. Get them to express their fears. Encourage team sports and modest risk-taking, but don't force them. They're impressionable and easy to manipulate. A positive manipulation, though, toward some kind of counseling may be a good idea. If you don't help them, they may stunt their own emotional growth. And because you're the parent, they'll probably blame you or your spouse later—if they don't already.

The Mender Boss

Mender bosses would rather file their own folders than criticize their secretaries. They don't want to risk your admiration, so they're easier to get along with than most bosses. But if you're doing a better job and get the same salary as the oh-so-imperfect person who works next to you, there's nothing you can do about it. That's because this boss won't want to cause any sort of conflict.

The Mender Employee & Friend

Mender employees will do everything humanly possible to be perfect. They'll also be your friends, covering your mistakes, driving you to work when your car's in the shop, babysitting your dog, bringing you flowers when you're sick and baking you a cake on your birthday. It might sound contradictory for a person who lacks emotional expression to overwhelm you with favors, but it's not. Menders don't have to get emotional in order to perform kind acts. Besides, if you're a Mender's friend, you're always listening to their problems, and so their good deeds may be an expression of their appreciation.

The Mender In-Law

Your Mender in-laws think you're either the best thing since the Dove Bar or the worst person since Mussolini—nothing in between. To get on their good side, lend a sympathetic ear, let them do you favors, and never allow them to know you're totally independent—especially if you are. However, if they try to take over parenting your children, you'll need to take a stand. Good luck.

I am trying to have a successful so with Servo Units and Electrodes. At time it is difficult but that it all the more enjoyable whenever success.

7. The Chameleon

On independence: It's your fault because I don't know what to do.
On thinking and feeling: I feel but I want to think.
On taking action: I leap-look-leap-crash.
On helping others: If I'm around, I'll help a little.
On love: I love you and you and you and you . . .

You've heard, "Jack of all trades, but master of none"? How about "rebel without a cause"? Both describe the unpredictable Chameleon. When you think you've got a Chameleon pegged, you're in for a big surprise. The Chameleon slant describes Chameleon personality—constantly changing direction. Oh, they're exciting all right. But they're also hypersensitive, moody, undisciplined, versatile, rigid, talented and utterly lacking in common sense. These are drastic words, but Chameleons are incredibly difficult people to understand, let alone love and trust and defend.

Chameleon is the Tarot's Fool card and Barrie's Peter Pan. These writers have their own idea of what reality is, and that isn't easy for others to comprehend.

They must be accepted on their own terms or not at all. Because they're so erratic, these terms may change on a daily basis. And that's confusing to the people closest to them. Chameleons will be affectionate one moment and hostile the next.

Another Chameleon hallmark is profound nonconformity. They must be accepted as rebels or not at all. They aren't going to be like you (unless you're a Chameleon reading this), and they don't want to be. They probably won't understand you either, because they tend to be self-involved.

Every graphologist for the past sixty years has labeled Chameleons with negative attributes. Chameleons have even been called socially inferior! But don't think they're criminals or lazy or bad people, just because they can't keep their slant straight. Call them eccentric. It's my opinion that Chameleons are flighty, but that they have many fine qualities, such as versatility and originality. They have exploring natures. And they reach out in every possible direction to understand the world.

There is much to love about a Chameleon. While it's true they are difficult to be with, significant growth can occur for you while you're with them. The only way to get along is for you to be super flexible and independent. Add this to the fact that you need to allow Chameleons to express their feelings without criticizing them. It takes strength to work things out with Chameleon, and you'll either develop that strength quickly or abandon the relationship.

Chameleons seem to know more about life than those who settle into routine existences. And that means they can be great fun, positive in outlook, cosmic in spirituality and highly sympathetic, because like their handwriting, they view life from many directions. These attributes could all work to their advantage — if Chameleons wanted them to.

Chameleons are usually inventive when they want things. For example, my Chameleon shopping buddy can trudge more miles through the fashion mart and persuade more sales people to discount than anyone I know. In fact, to this particular Chameleon, it's a major source of pride to be able to shop so brilliantly. I think she missed her calling. Instead of being a chiropractor, she should have been a buyer for a department store.

Chameleons are apt to be unorthodox business owners. For example, a Chameleon dentist I know runs his practice like a swap meet. He'll barter services, fill two cavities for the price of one, and pay a "finder's fee" to patients for referring other patients to him.

You as a Chameleon

Being a Chameleon, you may sometimes give people the wrong impression. While you're doing a good deed, you may be accused of insincerity, of having a hidden agenda and impure motives. You probably already know it's not easy to change a reputation once it's formed. In order to clear the slate, it may help to state exactly what you want out of a given situation. Then no one will mistake your intentions.

You have a very special kind of magic. While you accuse yourself of being too scattered, you neglect to take pride in the fact that you're able to diversify. Not many people could spread themselves so thin and remain creative individuals. You can, and you usually do it flawlessly.

Don't despair over being a Chameleon. Take pride in it. You're different, and that's terrific. You will probably never be satisfied with the status quo. Appreciate your versatility and ignore those who try to squeeze you into a mold in which you won't feel comfortable. Buy a three ring notebook to prioritize your projects and ideas. With an organized approach, you can inspire great changes in your world.

The Chameleon Mate

Keep an overview of the up and down cycles. When things are going well, appreciate the moments at hand. Try not to anticipate trouble, but accept the difficult times when they come. You'll have many good times and plenty of adventure. But don't expect Chameleons to change because you want them to. They do what they want to do, when they want to do it, and they will ignore your pleas that they change.

The Chameleon Child

If your children can't keep their slants going in one direction, you probably suspect someone switched babies before you left the hospital, and you're not alone. There are hundreds of parents like you who also tear out their prematurely gray hair. Just keep setting guidelines for your Chameleons and don't be manipulated by their tantrums. Get down on the floor and have one with them.

The Chameleon Boss

Chameleon bosses are generally difficult to work with because you don't know what to expect at any given moment. They probably have a desk somewhere beneath the piles of papers, and a "to do" list longer than two legal pads as well as a phone bill that could bankrupt AT&T. You'll need to put blinders on these bosses to keep them focused, so you'd better be organized yourself. But watch out that you're not manipulated into working every weekend.

The Chameleon Employee

If you're not careful, you may end up doing Chameleons' work for them. They're most charming when they want to be. And don't be flattered into trading workspace with them, or you could end up with a desk in the elevator.

How do you motivate a Chameleon to work? Through flattery, food or bribery.

The Chameleon Friend

Listen to what they say in your first conversations with them. They will let you know exactly who they are, so believe it. Could Cy Coleman, who wrote "Call Me Irresponsible," have been a Chameleon? If you want to go on a fishing trip with them, let it be a spur of the moment affair, because Chameleon plans almost invariably change when made in advance. Don't make any arrangements that require their commitment. They just might not be in the mood when the time comes.

The Chameleon In-Law

Don't play poker with a Chameleon in-law. There's more at stake than your ante, because Chameleons know that your poker persona reflects who you are in real life. And they may use their insights against you later.

Part 2
Compatibility Between Slanters

By this time you probably know which slant type you are and the slant types of the most important people in your life. Now you might be interested in considering how compatible they are with you—and with other people as well. The chapters in this section take the slanters one by one, starting with Thinker and ending with Chameleon, and examine every possible combination. But these combinations aren't repeated in each section. For example, if you're a Thinker, you only have to read the Thinker section. But if you're a Juggler, you would read the "Thinker-Juggler" section in the chapter "Thinker in Relationships," as well as the chapter on Jugglers.

Each chapter also discusses the major relationships: lover, sibling, friend, student or teacher, employee or employer. So if you're a Reactor and you want to find out about a romantic relationship with a Pleaser, let's say, you'd go to the "Pleaser in Relationships" chapter because the Pleaser chapter comes before the Reactor Chapter. Then find the section "Pleaser-Reactor" and read the "In Love" section.

Or suppose you are a Chameleon employee of a Mender. You'd go to the chapter called "Mender in Relationships," find the Mender-Chameleon heading, and read the "At Work" section.

STRIKING A MATCH

To say that any two people can create a great relationship sounds encouraging but may not be realistic. Because relationships are often fragile, certain conditions need to be met in order for romance or friendship to be productive. First, both people need to like themselves. Second, each person needs to accept the other—as is. Third, each one must enjoy being together more than going it alone.

As a graphologist, you can put together the most compatible of slants, but if those three conditions don't exist, any relationship could soon develop serious problems.

Someone who shares your slant will come closest to understanding you, because that person views the world as you do. You won't feel you're speaking in a foreign language. Next best is the slant closest to yours on the slant gauge. If you like challenge and opposites attract you, look for the slant two or more groups away.

8. Thinker in Relationships

THINKER-THINKER

In Love

You'd think that two Thinkers would truly value each other, and, of course, they would. They could discuss differences between Kant and Spinoza far into the night, and neither would get bored. Their gifts could range from "Trivial Pursuit" (the advanced edition) to Yugoslavian folk music tapes or matching binoculars for the opera.

They might view themselves as two logicians in a world of ill logic. And they are not about to fight, because Thinkers don't stoop to arguing—except about politics. Nor would two Thinkers fight over money, because neither would buy anything without consulting the other.

They might spend their entire lives in one apartment because they can't decide which house to buy. Thinkers don't like to gamble, and they dread the possibility of making a mistake with their money.

If they're in business together, there's a danger they will overwork and health will suffer as a result. They both tend to find their identity in their careers. More than any other couples, these two should plan regular vacations.

Thinkers aren't typically the cheating kind, but not for the reasons you'd think. They just don't want to expend any energy they don't absolutely have to. Unless they're very bored or unhappy with each other, they usually can rest assured that neither will be unfaithful, in mind—or in any other way.

Friends

The bars that show *Monday Night Football* on a big TV screen are filled with Thinker buddies. You see them toasting each other on *Cheers*, racing each other in 10K's in the rain, and you see them riding triple-loop roller coasters without letting out a single scream.

Two Thinkers may network and exercise together, but they should never become business partners. Neither one would want to go out to "cold call" or do the marketing end. Should the business go under, they might secretly blame each other for what went wrong. They would need a Juggler on board to make such a relationship work.

Siblings

Two Thinkers in the house might be fun if you enjoy why-did-the-chicken-cross-the-road jokes and *The Three Stooges* reruns every Saturday morning. They tend to get silly. The challenges they give each other are intellectual more than emotional. They're likely to remain best friends forever.

Teacher-Student

Since Thinkers are natural teachers, this would be a truly inspiring two-way relationship. If they didn't get along, it would be because each one would want to lead the class.

At Work

As co-workers, two Thinkers would be The Dynamic Duo. But if one is the boss, the relationship won't be terrific. If the underling Thinker is actually smarter than the boss, there will be resentment without confrontation. And if the boss has complaints about his Thinker employee, the situation may become volatile before anything is said. They need to schedule weekly grievance meetings.

THINKER-JUGGLER

In Love

Thinker likes Juggler's attitude that everything is okay and under control, because Thinkers feel they can relax when life is stable. But as we know, Juggler might be faking it. Nevertheless, Thinker sees Juggler as Someone to Believe In. Juggler is instinctively attracted by Thinker's no-nonsense nature. After all, Thinker seems to have true objectivity, which is the Juggler's lifetime goal.

By the time Thinker discovers that Juggler may indeed be unstable and over-emotional, it's too late: Thinker is in love. And when Juggler realizes Thinker's stability covers up indecisiveness, it's also too late. They've made a commitment, and they need to learn to accept each other's ways.

Thinkers try to stop Jugglers from fussing over little worries, but when Jugglers gloss over problems, they just store them up to suffer with later.

One answer is for Jugglers not to make any attempt to be as objective as Thinkers are. They must keep in touch with their emotions. For instance, Jugglers are apt to take things personally that actually have nothing to do with them. When this happens, they need to see the situation for what it is and let go of their inner anger, jealousy or resentment.

Being with Thinker can spur Juggler into overreacting. When Thinker refuses to take a stand against injustice, for example, Juggler may display enough fury for two in order to compensate for Thinker.

Learning quickly that Thinker refuses to fight, Juggler may feel impelled to take on the outside world single-handedly. For instance, if these two took their landlord to Small Claims court, Juggler would have to do all the talking. Only if they lost, would Thinker go into action. But Thinker's revenge might be sneaky. Remember that Thinkers aren't typically direct with their anger.

If Thinkers are instilled with enough guilt, religious or otherwise, they sabotage rather than confront directly. One Thinker I know, an altar boy, broke every window in a public school in the middle of the night. Another Thinker teenager (who got all A's in high school) stole cars. Both Thinkers had enormous hostility towards authority figures and since they couldn't confront anyone in particular, they acted out their anger toward everyone in general. Thinkers really need to learn to confront who and what they're angry with before they store up more rage than they can handle.

Thinkers and Jugglers are an excellent combination. They can absolutely change each other's lives for the better. (I know—because I'm a Juggler happily married to a Thinker.)

Friends

Juggler loves Thinker's self-reliance and self-control. Thinker admires Juggler's sense of adventure. This pair may go to wrestling matches together and argue with each other for decades about whether or not the matches are rigged. Their sense of humor will keep them together, and their friendship should last forever.

Siblings

If you suspect that your Thinker and Juggler kids hate each other, you're probably right, but they love each other, too. They dwell on each others' irritating habits, but then they also look up to each other.

If you catch Juggler sneaking out of the bedroom window, you can bet the sound-asleep Thinker put him up to it. When in doubt, blame the mastermind: the rebellious Thinker.

Teacher-Student

Thinker instructors are often Jugglers' mentors. It's a natural match. A Juggler can't lose if he follows in a Thinker's academic and professional footsteps.

At Work

Probably the very first old boys' network began with a Juggler and Thinker getting together. This is a wonderful match. On the job they will be extremely supportive of each other, but because Thinkers don't like to be told what to do, it's best if Thinker is the boss. If it's the other way around, it would be a good idea for Juggler to make suggestions rather than demands.

THINKER-PLEASER

In Love

JUGGLER: Why did you invite Jack for dinner for Saturday night? You know I invited Judy. And you were there when they broke up last month. How could you be so thoughtless?

THINKER: But they both like my lasagna. What's your problem?

If you're a Thinker—or a Pleaser—you already know you don't see eye-to-eye in everyday matters. You do not feel the same. You do not react the same. And you will probably struggle over your differences. But if you're the Thinker, you'd rather lace up your sneakers and go running than fight.

This is a common and rather popular combination, even though Thinkers and Pleasers are at almost opposite ends of the emotional spectrum. Each one has what the other lacks, but neither would want to trade places. Thinker rules his life with caution while Pleaser seems to live on impulse.

For the relationship to work well, Pleasers must understand that Thinkers, the essence of stability, aren't likely to change old habits. They could be married for ten years before Thinker would tell Pleaser that he really detests yams or anyone yelling orders from another room.

Pleasers must accept the fact that Thinkers aren't easily riled. They may dissolve in tears over the problems of ET, but real life situations won't seem to disturb them so much. Pleasers may believe that they'd like to be with a stable, comforting person, but when they spend time with Thinkers, they can't handle the monotony that accompanies the laid-back lifestyle. It's a trade-off.

Pleasers and Thinkers often can balance each other without compromising their basic values. But sometimes Pleasers try to manipulate Thinkers into emotional situations. And Thinkers are reluctant about being forced into scenes. They stammer and lose their voices. Thinkers don't use loaded words like "hate," "love" and "FANTASTIC!," and they don't know how to talk to angry Pleasers. This inspires Pleasers to pick an occasional fight, if only to ruffle Thinker feathers.

Pleasers need to allow Thinkers time to sort out feelings. They need more patience. Thinkers need to accept Pleasers' desires for immediate answers. They need to develop a greater sense of urgency.

Friends

Some Pleasers select only Thinker friends. Drawn to Thinker's apparent self-assurance, Pleasers become their great admirers. But when the first flush of friendship is over, they see each other's flaws all too clearly. The relationship is great while it lasts, and in many cases, they develop mutual respect and the friendship endures.

Siblings

Thinker children are absolutely certain their Pleaser siblings get good grades just to make them look bad.

Your Pleaser kids are going to be very affectionate and likely to grow up to enter a profession that serves others, such as social work, teaching or psychology. Your plotting and sometimes rebellious Thinkers may make you think they'll turn out to be bank robbers. But you're wrong. Thinkers outgrow (or adjust) their rebellious streak by the time they finish college, and Pleasers seldom begin to experience the full extent of their self-doubts until they're of voting age. By that time, they've all probably moved out of your house, and you won't reap the benefits of their maturity. But, rest assured, your Thinker will always be there for your Pleaser. And your Pleaser will always want to take care of Thinker, too—especially when Thinker gets the flu and needs nursing and chicken soup.

Teacher-Student

If Pleaser is the teacher, this will be a good learning experience. If Thinker is the teacher, it will be great. Pleasers invented bringing an apple to the teacher, and Thinkers invented eating. Good match.

At Work

Pleasers can drive Thinkers up the wall at work. Pleasers like more attention and reassurance than Thinkers want to give. And Pleasers don't let petty things go unnoticed, which irritates Thinkers.

For example, employee Pleaser gets furious at the custodian for not emptying his wastebasket for a whole week and complains to Thinker boss. Thinker doesn't want to deal with the custodian and ends up emptying the wastebasket himself every night so he doesn't have to listen to the griping.

THINKER-REACTOR

In Love

Reactors take great joy in rearranging the Thinker's world. They redecorate, move the furniture around monthly, invite strangers for dinner and switch the TV remote control every few minutes. If Thinkers are tolerant and easy-going (most are), Reactors may add a lot of fun to their lives. If Thinkers can't adjust to drastic changes, they won't be able to justify staying in the relationship.

Reactor wonders why Thinker dines at the same restaurants, sits in the same barber chair and sweats at the same health spa year in and year out. Reactor goes berserk without change, while Thinker enjoys living by a routine—a strict and serious routine. Each one won't understand what makes the other one tick, but with time, they may develop tolerance—maybe even fascination.

However, with Thinker watching such shows as *PBS Financial Reports* and Reactor watching *Dallas* and *Dynasty*, they may run into some static. If they don't learn to compromise, more serious issues will destroy their bond.

A major source of friction could be in their different needs for attention. Reactor needs approval and plenty of affection. Thinker could go for days without human contact. They need to understand this about each other, Thinker especially. Once Thinkers feel needed, they can be extraordinarily affectionate.

Friends

If Thinker gets divorced, Reactor may become more upset about it than Thinker. No problem is too remote for Reactor to fret over. Thinker may have to invent some problems just to keep Reactor happy. Generally, Thinkers like being fussed over by Reactors. And they also enjoy protecting them from the harsh side of life.

Siblings

Thinkers and Reactors both value family life. Reactors adore each and every family member—even when they hate them. Thinkers get along with even the most outrageous relations because they want to keep peace in the home.

Teacher-Student

Reactors make good teachers, especially in Montessori schools. They encourage Thinker students to be creative. But if Thinker is the teacher, and Reactor is the adoring, idolizing, restless student, Thinker may not know how to keep Reactor occupied and away from his desk. This is easily remedied by assigning complicated research projects to Reactor, who can handle them and love doing them.

At Work

How is Thinker going to get rid of Reactor long enough to get some work done? If Thinker is the boss, it's important to find some complex and time-consuming tasks. Reactors like being overly busy, they need to be needed and they usually are perfectionists. Reactors also need their own offices way way way down the hall.

With Reactor as the boss, Thinker has a more difficult time. Reactors are notorious for driving their subordinates at an insane pace, and Thinker will not function well under such conditions. Many Reactors tend to think that there's always more work to be done, and they don't know how to take it easy when they're in positions of authority.

THINKER-MENDER

In Love

You might think this is an unworkable combination. While Mender is happy with a small piece of the world (homelife), Thinker wants to feel like a part of the whole world. It might seem like *General Hospital* vs. *Sixty Minutes*. Over breakfast, Mender pores over Ann Landers while Thinker reads the editorials and business sections. They could share a newspaper beautifully, but how would they share a life?

Actually, this combination can be quite complementary. Thinker doesn't care about little details while Mender thrives on them. Mender worries about missing socks, a co-worker's allergies and the dog's skin condition, justifying it by saying, "What can I do about air pollution and nuclear war anyway?" But Thinker loves to dwell on earth-threatening issues. Together, they cover all bases. Nine out of ten times with this combination, the Mender is the female. Male Menders are rare.

As far as their emotional life is concerned, both are reserved, so neither would be apt to make impossible demands on the other. They both have a great potential for affection, however. How demonstrative they are depends upon other handwriting factors, such as spacing and size of lower loops, but we'll talk about those later.

Of course, if Mender becomes obsessed with knowing every single event in Thinker's past, it may annoy Thinker. And if Mender's phobias get out of hand, Thinker may become impatient with Mender's self-pity. And as Mender's self-pity increases, alienation from Thinker will also grow in direct proportion.

Some of Thinker's qualities, such as objectivity, intense loyalty, strong will and indifference to small catastrophes, might frustrate Menders. Menders may nag Thinkers to stand up for themselves and their families more often than they seem willing to do. Thinker's caution goes against taking strong stands, and Menders often feel they have to take on the entire outside world because Thinkers won't.

Since these slants are next to each other on the slant gauge, their potential for happiness is good, but be sure to take all the other handwriting traits into consideration, too.

As parents, Thinker and Mender can both be nurturing. Their children will probably feel very secure. However, if Thinker is overly concerned about the world and not the family, tears and tummy aches won't be able to compete with battles in Belfast. This means Mender might have to take over all the parenting. Because Menders usually enjoy their children depending on them, they don't object too much to this state of affairs. But it may cause their children to grow up expecting their mates—or their Mender parent—to take care of them.

Friends

A Thinker and Mender could very easily write a cook book or start a gourmet club together. In any case, their partnership would be a good idea. As long as they keep the relationship focused on a project, and not on an emotional track, they'll be quite happy together.

Siblings

The very best thing that could ever happen to Mender children is to have Thinker siblings. Who else would take the time to listen to them? A powerful lifelong bond may be forged here. And Thinkers will enjoy Mender admiration.

Teacher-Student

Mender coeds learn well with Thinker teachers, who probably wish all their students were Menders. Thinker teachers seem to be relaxed and pushovers for A's, but they aren't. Typical Menders won't walk into an exam unprepared or hand in a mediocre term paper. Therefore, Menders don't win popularity contests with the rest of their classes because they raise the grading curve.

Mender teachers demand scholastic excellence and Thinkers deliver it effortlessly. This encourages Mender teachers to challenge every student to be as good as the Thinker classmate, which, of course, makes the rest of the class jealous and angry.

Sometimes, however, Thinkers are smark alecks and show-offs in class. For example, a Thinker relative of mine was expelled for correcting the Spanish teacher. My Thinker husband admits to having antagonized the faculty when he flaunted a paperback Bible at school after his teacher banned paperbacks from the campus.

At Work

If the boss is the Thinker and Mender is the employee, this can be an excellent combination. Mender is quite content to stay behind the scenes and is supportive of the Thinker in all business activities. With Mender at the helm, it is also an excellent work combination, because Mender will support Thinker's networking and executive abilities.

THINKER-CHAMELEON

In Love

This pairing could be either the stuff of a murder mystery or a Goldie Hawn-Chevy Chase movie! To say they are vastly different personalities is an understatement. Their concerns are poles apart. Thinker worries about when the next issue of *Time* will arrive, while Chameleon isn't even sure it's still being published.

Thinker could demonstrate to Chameleon how a stable life is run, but Chameleon usually doesn't want one. Chameleons see too many unexplored possibilities to want to sit still. They reach out in all directions looking for what is new and exciting, expending a lot of energy while Thinkers try to conserve it. They could either drive each other crazy or complement each other very well. It all depends on whether or not they approve of each other in general.

Because Chameleons write with all the slants and therefore can relate to just about anything, they are certainly able to relate to Thinker objectivity. And Chameleons could possibly add adventure to the Thinker lifestyle. Chameleons are versatile and creative, and Thinkers can be too. Chameleons also might inspire Thinkers to try new activities, such as flying ultralights or getting a blackbelt in Tae Kwan Do.

For the union to be productive, Thinker needs to shed some of that stodginess and Chameleon needs to acquire common sense. If Chameleon goes too far in being unpredictable and unreliable, so that Thinker has to cover up mistakes and make excuses, Thinker may grow weary.

Children are quickly disillusioned by Chameleons, whose promises are often forgotten soon after they're made. Chameleons are apt to disappoint everyone—especially their kids. But they certainly are charming to children—especially when they talk about going on safari or hang gliding.

If the children recognize that they can rely totally on Thinker, they may be lenient toward Chameleon's behavior. But it's unlikely that they'll ever be immune to the disappointment that clouds most Chameleon relationships.

Friends

There won't be a great deal to keep these two together, unless it's a great deal of fun. Chameleons seem to bring out the daring in others. And they can certainly light fires under Thinkers. But Chameleons don't usually maintain lifelong friendships. They change addresses too often.

Siblings

What's the difference between a Thinker and a Chameleon child? Well, you'll know for sure when a Chameleon has done something "bad." Thinkers are better sneaks and aren't often caught. Tommy and Dick Smothers are such a combination. Guess which is which. (If you think you're right, you're wrong! The "dumb" one is the Thinker!)

Teacher-Student

If it's an art or craft class, the teacher will be the Chameleon who will probably believe Thinker is too right-brained to create anything. If the subject is academic, Thinker is at the dais and won't appreciate Chameleon's wisecracks.

At Work

If they're both in sales, Thinker can learn much from Chameleon about telemarketing and getting good referrals. If it's a 9 to 5 job, Chameleon won't be there long enough to get on Thinker's nerves.

Because Chameleon handwriting sometimes resembles Thinker handwriting, they have great potential for working well together. They will understand each other at very basic levels. However, it's almost impossible for Chameleons to pull manipulative shenanigans on Thinkers, because Thinkers are smarter than Chameleons think.

A case in point: A Chameleon construction worker I know tried to get her Thinker boss to send her to Alaska to learn to build igloos. She said they could then make a fortune specializing in constructing geodesic domes. Think he fell for it?

9. Juggler in Relationships

JUGGLER-JUGGLER

In Love

Two Jugglers will compete for the Nice Mate of the Year award.
"After you."
"No, after you, my dear."
"But I insist. After you."

Jugglers want to be perfect, and they want it now. Not only that, they want everyone else to be perfect, too. And since no one will ever be perfect, the two Jugglers will undoubtedly be dissatisfied with themselves and with each other. They need to realize that striving for perfection is irrational.

When Jugglers run into diffculties, it's important for them to talk to each other and not behind each other's back. Their tendency to avoid confrontation often keeps them from doing this. It forces them into secret alliances and always works against them. Holding things back will not hold them together. Talking about feelings clears the air. In fact, it's the only thing that works. If they can't talk about their feelings together, they need help.

If the Jugglers come together *only* to solve problems, though, skies still won't be rosy. Why? Because they're setting up a dependent relationship. If one or both of them do succeed in solving their problems, the reason to stay together will be gone. Two Jugglers must be best friends in order to be best lovers. They need regular tete-a-tetes and plenty of affection. Problems may bring them face to face, but they need successes to cement them together.

When Jugglers get together for the right reasons, integrating their emotional needs and logical natures, they're a fabulous combination. They also have a great potential for sexual attraction, because the same things turn them on.

Above all else, two Jugglers need to keep their romance alive. They tend to get too busy and neglect the passion that brought them together. So, it's a great idea for them to make dates with each other, as if their relationship were still brand new and their feelings were still urgent. When their lovelife gets lustreless or unsatisfying, it's important for them to take a break from daily routine and rekindle those old feelings. Romantic weekend get-aways are an excellent prescription.

Friends

About half of the population of our society writes with a Juggler hand. And they believe the other half wishes it did, too. When two Jugglers get together, you've got two high achievers trying to outperform each other. While they're competing they should keep in mind that their friendship is more important than the pride they have at stake. And since Jugglers are always overly busy, they need to make time for each other. Then they can be great friends.

Siblings

Two Juggler children make for a highly competitive household. They carry on the classic Juggler internal conflict: Is it better to be logical or emotional? Wise parents will help them develop scholastically, physically (with sports) and emotionally by helping them label and discuss feelings, as they try to find their own answers to the puzzle.

Teacher-Student

This is a splendid scholastic combination—even if student Jugglers do think they're smarter than teacher Jugglers. A good ongoing supportive relationship could arise for the student.

At Work

Jugglers don't work well under other Jugglers. They're too close in temperament not to get on each other's nerves. And they recognize all the traits they don't like about themselves in the other. They should work as independently as possible, and try to keep criticism to a minimum.

JUGGLER-PLEASER

In Love

This is the most popular combination, and with good reason. Jugglers gain emotional insight by watching Pleasers operate, while Pleasers gain objectivity by observing Jugglers. They each need what the other has, and if both are willing to grow and put plenty of love into the relationship, they can get plenty of love out of it.

Pleasers are unafraid of passionate love and the future. Jugglers are skeptical of the very words "love" and "future," but they can get into both passion and planning through Pleaser's example.

Jugglers help keep Pleasers down to earth with their reserve and the ability to seek moderation. Excess seems vulgar to Jugglers, and to satisfy them, Pleasers learn to curb their impulsiveness and their appetites. Jugglers may not be cheapskates exactly, but they are practical with their generosity as a rule.

Inspired Jugglers may wine and dine Pleasers (whether Juggler is male or female) until they both gain ten pounds. Juggler may try to win Pleaser with thoughtful little gifts, attention and time—at least at the beginning of the relationship. And also at the beginning, Juggler will do anything to keep Pleaser happy. Well, maybe anything. Juggler won't want to be fondled in public, for example. Jugglers can be as Teddybearish as any Pleaser, but they prefer to demonstrate affection in private.

Pleasers admire Juggler objectivity. It isn't as black and white as Thinker objectivity, because Jugglers don't stick rigidly to one ideal for a whole lifetime. They're more openminded, or at least more open to change than Thinkers. This is what makes them so desirable to a Pleaser.

Pleasers need to take care not to press Jugglers into corners, because Jugglers generally would rather walk than fight. When rationality gives way to frustration, Jugglers may go for the jugular. For example, let's say Pleaser nags Juggler to ask for a raise, but Juggler is afraid to do it. After two months of being pestered day and night, Juggler might just throw a brick through the picture window. Pleasers may need to handle some dramatic outbursts.

Jugglers need to be concerned with the tender feelings of a Pleaser. Pleasers are extremely sensitive, especially to criticism. So if Jugglers want to complain, they need to be gentle and clear.

Pleasers *demand* loyalty, so Jugglers had better be sure they want to make a commitment before they get involved. Jugglers tend to be fickle, especially during their twenties, and sometimes they can be as impulsive as Pleasers. But if they play with Pleaser emotions, they are likely to have to deal with more than they bargained for.

Only a few degrees separate Pleaser and Juggler slants, but those degrees reveal a great difference in the way they react to life and to each other. Understanding that difference, and respecting it, is the key to making life a rich experience together. This is a good combination for raising children if the parents are sensitive to each other.

Friends, Siblings, Teacher-Student and At Work

You're talking about average handwriting when you're talking about Pleasers and Jugglers living and working under the same roof. Generally speaking, if both Juggler and Pleaser are positive in outlook, they will have great potential for getting along. If both are negative, almost any relationship will be difficult. But because these are the two most common slants, and there are also two kinds of Jugglers and two kinds of Pleasers, you need to look at quite a few other handwriting traits in order to evaluate these relationships.

JUGGLER-REACTOR

In Love

If Juggler can handle huge amounts of intense affection and utter devotion, Reactor will spoonfeed it. If Reactor can handle Juggler's occasionally evasive ways and sporadic displays of affection, the relationship may work. There are many trade-offs for this pair.

Reactors "know" the passionate life is the only life worth living and they dance to their heart's music. This makes most Jugglers nauseous. Only if the Juggler can joyously join this "dance" will the relationship satisfy both. And Juggler may need to be convinced again and again that it's all right to get so deeply involved with another person.

Reactors must come to respect the Juggler need for privacy and not expect the intensity of a new relationship to last forever. Unrealistic expectations on Reactor's part could tear the two apart. Ultimately, in any case, Reactor might get offended (or at best bored) with Juggler's frequent indifference to passion. On the flip side, Juggler must realize that Reactor truly needs constant attention, affection and time, time, time. The Relationship is Everything to Reactor.

Life will be exciting and intense for this pair. Very intense. Reactor supplies their life with countless projects. One Reactor I know is President of the PTA, starting two new businesses, teaching Sunday school, and vividly aware of what's going on behind every door in the neighborhood.

Another Mrs. Reactor sewed costumes for a whole ballet troupe, constructed a jungle gym, fixed the car on the freeway shoulder, camped out on the living room floor instead of taking a vacation and reshingled the roof—amazing energy! Her Juggler husband ran his own business and provided emotional stability for the family. That's a great match, and they're known for having a drop-around-anytime home.

The Juggler-Reactor combination works best when the Jugglers know what they want out of life. And it's also on Juggler's shoulders to determine if the relationship is worth the effort, because Reactor's vision is usually clouded by emotion. This is where Juggler's Thinker abilities come in handy.

The children of this relationship will have lots of fun, but Reactors aren't happy when they go away to college. Reactors often become centered on their family and have major adjustments to make when the children leave. Unless they turn their energy toward their mates and to new projects, they may feel as if their lives are over.

Friends

Reactors and Jugglers can be good friends if they don't see each other very often. Because they're both busy people, they'll have plenty to say when they finally make room for each other in their schedules. They have the potential for an excellent friendship, because they both may come to care a great deal about each other's welfare.

Siblings

Juggler and Reactor children are just about guaranteed not to like each other when they're young. Reactor spends more time on the phone than an AT&T operator. And Juggler may want to start his own business by the time he's in high school. Sound like Mallory and Alex on *Family Ties?* They do love each other, though, in spite of their differences.

Teacher-Student

With Juggler as student, and Reactor as a *talented* teacher, a truly inspiring atmosphere can develop. But if it's the other way around, Juggler won't want Reactor constantly hanging around his desk.

At Work

If Juggler boss has a private workspace, a tolerable relationship may develop with a Reactor employee. Tolerance is about the most you can expect with this combination, because Reactors need to manufacture tension when things are fine. That will annoy Juggler who simply wants to work. When you find a Juggler and Reactor in a good working relationship, look for other positive handwriting aspects, such as narrow letters and wide spacing between them. (See The Compatibility Test on page 194.)

A Reactor boss wants more control than Juggler can stand. It isn't an easy relationship, but it can work if Juggler is given creative freedom and a flexible work schedule so their paths don't cross every hour. If that's not possible, they should keep their distance. I know of Reactor employees who have driven their Juggler co-workers to resign—and their Juggler bosses to move to other floors!

JUGGLER-MENDER

In Love

Jugglers have the least need for socializing of all the right slant types, while Menders come by reclusiveness naturally. So these two can be quite happy and satisfied with each other. If they both want to have children, the relationship can really flourish; they're apt to get bored without a major shared interest.

I know a Juggler-Mender couple who has been married for 24 years, and by most people's standards, they have a wonderful relationship. For one thing, they share many interests. They do volunteer work for American Field Service; they are avid restaurant goers, and they enjoy taking care of their grandson together. The key to their happiness is that the Juggler learned to tolerate the Mender's preoccupation with little details and her intense interest in other people's lives. The Mender developed tolerance toward the Juggler's instant empathy for a wide variety of people, his dislike of details and his fondness for exciting new things. And they both were willing to work through the difficult times.

Jugglers and Menders find it easy to appreciate each other's talents.

Menders are marvelous at following up on details, tending to children's needs and really caring for the people in their lives. Jugglers excel at overseeing big projects, planning ahead and making peace among troublemakers.

Friends

This is a popular friendship, probably because Jugglers need the care and attention that Menders dispense so freely, while Menders receive ideas and encouragement that expand their universe.

The pitfall here is for the Mender to complain to the Juggler. Jugglers usually have a no-nonsense approach to problems: solve them or forget them. This is heresy to a Mender, who would rather complain than cure. If this is the case, Juggler needs to say, "I enjoy your company, but when I hear so many complaints, I get fidgety and frustrated." If Menders care enough about keeping the friendship going, they should try to set up a positive frame of mind when visiting Juggler and swap complaints with a Pleaser or Reactor friend.

Siblings

Jugglers, as you know, struggle to be more logical than emotional. But with a Mender sibling around, the Juggler probably will not have to struggle much. That's because Mender children are emotional, self-conscious and timid, and that makes Jugglers feel strong. That strength may turn into protectiveness for the Mender's benefit. So if they love each other, they will encourage each other all the way to maturity.

Teacher-Student

What a marvelous learning experience this is! Both have innate scientific and creative interests. They could come up with new ideas that benefit the world, because when you're talking about Menders and Jugglers, you're talking about practical and altruistic people who get things done.

At Work

Since Menders like to take care of details but generally dislike supervising, and Jugglers like to make big plans and may be excellent supervisors, these two can become a wonderful workteam. The editor of my newspaper column is a Mender, and we have an excellent working relationship. She also seems to manage quite well as the supervisor of a small staff. Whatever each person's talents are, they can work well together.

JUGGLER-CHAMELEON

In Love

No one could possibly understand and cope with a Chameleon better than a Juggler. The question is whether a Juggler would want to invest that kind of time and energy! The bottom line for Juggler is whether the relationship is worth what it takes to maintain it. Chameleon doesn't know what bottom line means.

If Jugglers finally succumb to the Chameleons' line and fall in love (against their better judgment), Chameleons can actually methodically drive Jugglers insane. Quickly discovering the Juggler's most vulnerable point, Chameleons harp on that weak spot, until the Jugglers indeed begin to question their mental health. It's all over when Jugglers see this form of mental abuse for what it is. They will likely leave the relationship, because they're much too straightforward and honest to want to play mind games.

Juggler likes to evaluate situations, and then—evaluate them all over again. "Let's look at the facts from all possible sides," says Juggler. When faced with Chameleon, whose approach is continually shifting, forcing even more evaluation, Juggler is thrown off balance. Juggler may ultimately decide that the relationship is not worth working on.

Friends

"Hunting season started, Jug, old boy, want to go tomorrow?"
"Can't, Cham, have to go to work."
All Jugglers could use at least one Chameleon friend. While Jugglers find it difficult to have fun, Chameleons have trouble delaying it. They're good for each other!

Siblings

If the original brothers were literate, Cain would have been a Chameleon, and Abel would have been a Juggler. Get the picture? This isn't to say your Chameleon child is going to murder your Juggler child. It's just a warning that the Chameleon may diabolically get the Juggler into trouble.

Teacher-Student

If Juggler were the teacher, he'd flunk Chameleon. If Chameleon were the teacher, Juggler would get all A's. But then Chameleon would give A's to everyone.

At Work

This will be an excellent workteam if Chameleon uses that innate, uncanny ability to perceive what Juggler and other workmates need and want to hear—especially if Chameleon is the boss. With Juggler as the boss, both must be sensitive to the fact (and take into account) that they have entirely different work habits. If the results are satisfactory, they should forgo quibbling over the methods to each other's madness.

10. Pleaser in Relationships

PLEASER-PLEASER

In Love

This match is very much like Juggler-Pleaser, but two Pleasers are far more frisky. They're also more spontaneous, creative, energetic and totally unafraid of deep feelings. This pair in love is inspiring to all of us. Of course, other factors enter in, such as, which types of Pleaser are we talking about? Insecure types or heart-centered, loving types? But having the Pleaser slant in common is a great place to start.

To Pleasers, there's no such thing as having too much money. Especially when spacing is wide between letters and words, they'll love to spend money on each other, on cooking gadgets, on food and word processors, VCRs, condos, Club Med, scuba in Aruba, primitive sculptures, original Dalis and everything else. They will generally spend money as fast as possible. If MasterCard only knew—it would conduct special promotions to sponsor these marriages.

On a deeper level, the way this couple spends money is a reflection of how they spend energy on each other. They put extraordinary vitality into the relationship to make it work. They also share a zest for life and for each other that few couples experience. *This is true only if both Pleasers have generous spacing between letters and if they're basically heart-centered.*

Pleasers enjoy a good fight every now and then because they enjoy making up. But it's important they not say things that are impossible to take back. They also need to be careful *not* to make each other jealous. A jealous Pleaser can make life miserable for the offender, because they aren't the best forgive-and-forgetters.

The children of Pleasers often try the patience of their teachers, because they expect other people to think they're as cute as their families do. They are happiest at progressive schools where they can express themselves freely—anytime, anywhere and over anything!

Friends

Probably half the friendships in the English, Spanish, Portuguese and French-speaking world are of this combination, because most people write with the Pleaser slant. Two Pleasers will make plenty of time in their lives for socializing. They won't tend to lose track of each other as some other types will, and the bonds they create may become deep.

Siblings

Insecure Pleaser siblings will fight and be very jealous of each other. The heart-centered type will develop a lifelong devotion. Neither kind is above tattling on the other.

Teacher-Student

Most student-teacher relationships are made up of this combination, because most people were taught to write with a Pleaser slant. (Remember your third grade teacher's handwriting chart?) So this slant reflects the average educational relationship, based on Pleaser values. Actually, a typical Pleaser career *is* teaching, and most teachers have good intentions, affection for their students and a desire to help them learn.

At Work

The relationship could be excellent, but it depends on the type of Pleasers you're analyzing. If they're both the heart-centered type, the work atmosphere may be inspiring. But if they are insecure and react from a sense of inferiority, the competition and jealousy may overwhelm them. At the heart of many office problems you'll find an insecure Pleaser causing trouble by spreading rumors and asking co-workers to take sides in petty issues.

PLEASER-REACTOR

In Love

It seems wonderful at first; Pleasers think Reactors will make all their romantic dreams come true. No one can love Pleaser more than Reactor. "How long may I rub your feet, darling?" "Will you let me write that report for you?" "When can I wash your car?"

Will it last? If Pleaser feels worthy of royal treatment, it just might!

Actually, Pleaser is the only type that can fully appreciate Reactor. That's because Reactor lavishes such wild affection on a lover that their behavior tends to make anyone else suspicious. Pleasers have always wished that all the care and attention they've spent so extravagantly on others would come back to them. Well, it's paid back in spades by Reactor.

Many a Pleaser-Reactor couple spend 24 hours a day together. They inhale and exhale in unison. They couldn't imagine having separate friends because they don't enjoy doing anything without each other.

Will problems arise? If Pleaser desires independence, being with Reactor might make this need more urgent. Pleaser may become frustrated with Reactor's emotional dependence, and feel smothered and overwhelmed. Reactor's excessive romanticism can't be overlooked. When they don't feel appreciated, Reactors may mope around the house for days.

Their kids are tremendously well-loved. The devotion this pair feels for each other spreads and encompasses the whole family. They go camping, hiking and amusement-parking together. One problem their kids might face? The outside world probably will never seem as loving as the Pleaser-Reactor home, and it may be difficult for these children to accept the idea that there are other kids in the classroom, when they're used to being the center of their parents' universe.

Friends

Pen Pals Of The Year award goes to this pair. They will communicate until they get writer's cramp. Their phone bills to each other will be staggering. The only hope is that they'll live close enough to meet, but far enough away to keep out of each other's daily routine.

Siblings

Pleaser might see Reactor as a big baby, an overly romantic idiot or a great friend. Reactor will adore Pleaser, no matter what, at least while they're growing up. But they will never feel neutral about each other, because they're both such passionate creatures.

Teacher-Student

There will be a passion for learning no matter which one is the student.

At Work

Let's face it. Reactors need to be isolated because they can talk so much no one will get any work done. But if they have to share an office with anyone, let it be a Pleaser. Pleaser may be the only one who can handle it without resentment.

A Pleaser boss will value Reactor efficiency, but may get annoyed if Reactor escalates social tension in the office by snooping in others' business.

A Reactor boss will emotionally identify with a Pleaser employee and assume the whole staff wants to have a comfortable, homey office. But don't let framed, smiling faces on Reactor's desk fool you. Reactors run tight ships and want ultimate authority over all work that leaves their departments.

PLEASER-MENDER

In Love

This couple's dynamic depends on how well Mender accepts Pleaser's intensity, and to what extent Pleaser accepts Mender's subdued ways of expressing feelings. Pleasers are extroverted while Menders stay behind the scenes. Pleasers thrive on action and problem-solving, while Menders are more reserved and don't always want to solve their problems. Both desire approval, even if Menders don't admit it. How could these two get along?

It can work if the Pleasers are able to give the Menders the sense of emotional security that they require. If the Pleasers feel appreciated and understood, that will not be difficult. Often Mender caution may temper Pleaser impulsiveness, while Pleaser lust for life can tug Mender out into the world. And Menders can be a lot of fun, when they're not focused on their problems. If both operate at their best, they'll have a fine time together. If they don't, the going gets tougher.

If the Pleaser insists on dragging the Mender out of the security of the home, the Mender might feel inadequate and manipulated. The Mender might start dwelling on personal vendettas and get socially paralyzed. If the Pleaser isn't carrying on the same feud, these attitudes will be depressing.

If Pleaser becomes thoroughly depressed by Mender, their kids may start playing "Cheering Up The Folks." This game challenges all participants, and no one ever wins. The kids won't be able to fix their parents' lives or their marriage. But like most kids, they'll feel that the problem is their fault and keep trying. When they move away from home, they may go on to connect with depressed mates who will keep the game going with another set of Unsolvable Problems.

This relationship is a difficult one because Pleasers and Menders are such different personalities. They need to work diligently on understanding each other.

Friends

PLEASER: What do you want to do today?

MENDER: Let's go to the museum.

PLEASER: But we went there last week. I'd rather go to that psychic Jenny told us about.

What's happening here? Menders are fascinated with the past and Pleasers want to know about the future so they can plan for it. When they don't agree on important issues, they need to compromise. Pleasers usually compromise anyway. But they need to make sure they aren't manipulated into compromising, because Menders can easily push Pleasers to act out of a sense of guilt.

Siblings

Because the Pleasers' goal is popularity, and the Menders' is peace and quiet, these two are not likely to become best friends. Seldom will they share a hobby. The best you can hope for is mutual respect. As adults, they probably will not see each other more than twice a year. And if they really don't like each other, there's no reason why they should try to force a relationship between them to work.

Teacher-Student

If Menders are the teachers, they won't understand Pleasers' impulsive ways and far-out ideas. But if Pleasers are the teachers, they may be able to get Menders to expand their thinking. When Pleasers pick up on Mender fascination with the past and history, they can encourage the student to use that talent for research.

At Work

Pleasers will want to rush through projects just to get them out ahead of time, while Menders will want to pick and repick through them to make sure they're perfect. Will they drive each other crazy? It depends on who is boss. Pleaser boss will either force Mender employee to pick up the tempo or pick up an unemployment check. Mender Boss may temper Pleaser's impulsiveness by being a role model of careful planning and forethought.

PLEASER-CHAMELEON

In Love

Pleasers crave security, passion and creativity. They need to be recognized and appreciated. Chameleons appreciate but only in spurts. They're spurty kinds of people. Chameleons may feel guilty for not being able to supply praise and adoration continually. If the Pleasers are secure in themselves, however, constant approval won't be necessary, and Chameleons won't have to feel guilty. That's the key. If the Pleasers can handle it, Chameleons can teach them some vital lessons. By giving Pleasers plenty of time alone, Chameleons allow them the chance to develop self-reliance and self-approval. They can teach Pleasers that they don't have to depend on others for praise, because the most valuable praise comes from within. And, of course, Pleasers—never as dependent as Reactors for external praise—will be able to build up their self-confidence as a result.

The Chameleon sense of adventure and drama adds excitement to any union. One notable Oregon Chameleon is a psychic surgeon, set designer and farmer. He is almost always traveling. His Pleaser mate has no problem with his leaving on short notice, because she has learned to appreciate her time alone. It took diligence and many lonely nights, but the result is an independent, self-sufficient woman.

Children make Chameleons feel guilty. Chameleons want to spend Quality Time with them, but there are so many distractions in Chameleons' lives that their promises are often broken. This is sad for everyone involved. Pleasers end up making excuses for Chameleons, and no one wins.

If Chameleons make honest efforts to become more stable, things can work out. Children can feel secure and develop normally. But in order for this union to work for the children, Pleaser has to be emotionally strong and accept the fact that Chameleon probably will be unreliable and can't really help it. Chameleon needs to accept the fact that Pleaser will overcompensate to some degree, spending too much money on the children's clothes, circus tickets and cello lessons.

Friends

Even though these two might not have a thing in common, they'll be fascinated with each other's lives. This may not be a lifelong friendship, but it will be fun while it lasts.

Siblings

Pleasers' rooms are generally neat and clean. These kids may even request a special organizing system for their closets. Chameleons' rooms look as if the Governor should be called in to declare them disaster areas.

Chameleons don't feel at home in Pleasers' rooms, let alone with Pleasers' friends, projects and sport preferences. These creatures are from different planets. They may like each other or plot against each other, but they won't be indifferent.

Teacher-Student

Only a Pleaser teacher would have the patience to cope with a smart aleck Chameleon in the classroom, and the Pleaser might even be able to inspire Chameleon with way-out projects. A Chameleon teacher is likely to stretch the Pleaser's imagination.

At Work

Chameleons make extraordinary challenges for Pleasers, who need a neat, orderly workspace. Chameleons think that neat desks are indicative of mental disorderliness. Pleasers think that messy desks mean messy thinking. (Not that all Pleasers are tidy, but most are.)

If Chameleon boss acts helpless, Pleaser employee will come to the rescue. This relationship has a few disadvantages, especially if Chameleon takes advantage of Pleaser's good nature. Then, too, Pleasers can sabotage Chameleons just by not concealing the fact that they came in to work late, left early, misplaced the file cabinet keys, drank a five martini lunch and and so on and so on.

If Pleaser is the employer, Chameleon will either manipulate special favors or get fired after two months. Most likely, Pleaser will need Chameleon's talents desperately in order to put up with all the shenanigans that come with this work relationship. There's always an excuse (some sounding more valid than others) with Chameleon around.

11. Reactor in Relationships

REACTOR-REACTOR

In Love

Reactors overrespond, overreact, and are overly affectionate. If both Reactors overrespond, overreact, and are overly affectionate simultaneously, this relationship can be successful, but that takes a lot of planning. This isn't an ideal match, but it may be comforting for a Reactor to be with someone who understands what it's like to be so intense.

If the Reactors like themselves, they will probably like each other. If not, the union holds no hope. It's sad, but if Reactors don't accept their own impulsive, dependent and thin-skinned nature, they won't accept it in someone else.

It's highly unlikely that two Reactors would ever meet. If they did, it's doubtful that they would fall in love. For one thing, they both need enormous amounts of attention. They aren't likely to satisfy each other's needs, because they're too busy trying to satisfy their own. For another thing, the energy of one Reactor is hard to bear. The energy of two Reactors could supply enough power to light the city of New York for a month. Simply put, they may overwhelm each other and everyone around them, like two hurricanes colliding.

Friends

These two would never get to see each other because they'd never be able to hang up the phone on each other. If they fight, they may hold a grudge for years but still never stop loving one another.

Siblings

Peace and tranquility will not visit the home of two Reactors very often. Unless these two are twins and adore each other, they should have their own rooms at opposite ends of the house—just because they are so intense. They should also have their own phones, own friends and if possible, go to different schools. Good luck.

Teacher-Student

Because Reactors are intense about everything they do, their shared educational experience might inspire brilliant work. It would be fortunate, though highly unlikely, for two Reactors to be in this relationship. If the teacher is older, the student may feel more completely understood than ever before. This combination is highly emotional, but it can be terrific!

At Work

Two Reactors in the same office may drive everyone to look for another job. Or the Reactors may leave everyone else alone and communicate only with each other. Or they may hate each other passionately and never speak to each other at all. How can you determine which way the relationship will go? You can't, because Reactors base their decisions solely on their feelings, and it's difficult to say what will rub them the right or wrong way.

REACTOR-MENDER

In Love

Friends, relatives and neighbors will wonder how this couple ever got together. Their outlooks are so different, you wouldn't think they'd have a hope of understanding each other.

While Mender might be busy with the scout troop, tending to sick relatives and defleaing the dog, Reactor might be involved with every networking group in town, as well as Greenpeace and Save the Earth societies.

This is a strange combination. Reactor is *extremely* outgoing, extroverted and dependent on others. Mender is reclusive and *extremely* introverted. They'd be each other's biggest challenge and probably have a lifelong tug-of-war. If the relationship does succeed, it will be because they admire each other for what they themselves lack. All too often though, people are attracted to their opposites only to discover they'd prefer to be with someone more like themselves.

Friends

In most cases, this will be a very casual relationship, and they won't want to spend a great deal of time together. They won't have much in common, and their mutual respect is apt to be minimal.

Siblings

A Mender and a Reactor under the same roof might be fun, but there is a danger that Reactor will steal all the attention. Menders don't readily ask for what they need to be happy, and they may become resentful toward the popular Reactor. Because these two are so drastically different, they may admire or else be insanely jealous of each others' innate talents and potentialities. It's almost as though they act out each other's fantasies. Reactor likes to imagine feeling comfortable being alone in a room reading a book. Mender may daydream of being the life of the party.

Teacher-Student

The relationship between these two won't last longer than one semester, unless the teacher is a Reactor who can appreciate the careful research the Mender puts into all projects.

At Work

Neither would be the other's mentor, but they might work well together. While Menders enjoy being part of a team, Reactors will probably get impatient with nit-picking details. It's advisable then for them to divide up the tasks so both are doing what they do best. Reactor should be the planner, and Mender should check for mistakes.

A Reactor boss will appreciate a Mender employee's dedication and willingness to work overtime. A Mender boss won't understand a Reactor's frequent emotional emergencies and moodiness, but will probably be sympathetic.

REACTOR-CHAMELEON

In Love

It's an unlikely combination, but it just might work, if the relationship is based on love and not dependence. They do share a passion for life and for adventure. And they need to keep in mind that they'll never succeed in changing each other.

If you read the previous chapter carefully, it won't surprise you when I say that Reactor and Chameleon "in love" is an immediate contradiction. It should read Reactor and Chameleon "in dependence." These two lost souls are searching for the cosmic mommy, each hoping that the other will fulfill their destiny.

Is it hopeless? Not necessarily.

If Chameleon enjoys life and has done plenty of work on getting goals together, he or she might be able to make Reactor happy. This is probably the only way a healthy relationship could develop. But usually Chameleon is too absorbed in personal problems to be able to give Reactor enough attention.

Reactor, of course, will be a more nurturing parent than Chameleon, though neither are calm and emotionally reliable people. If they are considering having children, they might think about postponing if for a couple of years until they can get to know and love each other more deeply. In the meantime, pets are fun, too! How about getting a boa constrictor or a monkey to raise?

Friends

Even though these two might not have any mutual interests, they are likely to be fascinated by each other. They might even be best buddies for a year or so, but it's unlikely they would have enough in common to be friends permanently.

Siblings

Reactor children live to please their parents. Chameleon children live to please themselves and anyone else they want to impress. Both groups think their real siblings were switched at the hospital. I know of a couple of extreme cases that spend their lives looking for that "real" brother or sister.

Reactors sometimes blame Chameleons for "forcing" them to live in an emotionally disrupted house. And Chameleons usually have some gripes, too. This combination can live peacefully together, but it takes patience (and often counseling) to achieve it.

Teacher-Student

Neither has patience when dealing with the other. Student Chameleons are likely to turn in cola-stained reports, or none at all, which may or may not amuse the Reactor. It depends on Reactor's mood at the time. Teacher Reactors might never be able to get Chameleons to construct an orthodox paragraph, let alone untangle the mysteries of conjugation.

At Work

If they work in separate offices in separate cities, they may be able to talk to each other on the phone. These two have completely different workstyles, and they'd probably never complete a project together without wanting to murder each other—no matter which is the boss and which is the employee. Both are moody—but for different reasons. Reactor attacks new projects impulsively. Chameleon wants to be free to hop from one project to another and won't be pinned down to Reactor's timetable. That drives a conscientious Reactor up the wall.

I know a Reactor pottery store owner who has been trying for years to supervise his Chameleon employee. If Chameleon isn't behind the kiln taking a nap or smoking a cigarette, he makes planters when the boss wants mugs. They throw more tantrums than pots around there. Neither one is happy.

12. Mender in Relationships

MENDER-MENDER

In Love

Can two people who live in fear of the future live in bliss? Yes. They can share the love of creating a family, involvement in community affairs, the fun of cooking up exotic dishes and other things, too. Two Menders won't make emotional demands on each other and definitely will not pick on each other. This couple will respect each others' privacy (and phobias) in order to create an emotionally safe home. They'll also satisfy each other socially, because they're both homebodies. Neither will ask the other to go out dancing. If you find an exception to that little rule, it's probably the Mender woman who gets in the mood to dance.

Sharing life goals, having similar attitudes toward raising children and holding major philosophies in common may be all they need to lead meaningful lives together. They may also find that church, temple or community involvement adds meaning to their lives. Or perhaps just a comfortable home, a few friends and a close family is all they need to be happy.

Friends

It's highly unlikely that two Menders would find each other and become friends. It's usually an outgoing Pleaser or Juggler who makes the initial contact with a Mender. But when Menders discover each other, they have so much in common that they really enjoy each other's company.

Siblings

A Mender family member may turn out to be everyone's scapegoat. Sensitive, easily upset and vulnerable, they're easy to tease. Usually only family members know how unsteady Menders are, and they make fun of the Mender for taking things too seriously. Of course, this only causes Mender to retreat even further into a private fantasy world. If there are two Menders in the house, they'll take refuge in each other's company.

Teacher-Student

This relationship is excellent, especially if what's being taught is craft- or art-related. And after the course ends, they might become close friends.

At Work

A Mender-Mender work relationship will often develop into a deep friendship, even if one of the Menders is the boss. The only danger with this combination at work is that they may get so obsessed over details that they won't move forward. They should add a Juggler to this team to develop new ideas and formulate future plans.

I've heard wonderful things about Mender bosses. People say they're fair, they want to be liked and accepted by their employees, and they're generous. I've never heard of a Mender boss with a Mender supervisor, but I imagine it would be a pleasant and comfortable relationship.

MENDER-CHAMELEON

In Love

Mender puts socks and undies in the drawers by color in

alphabetical order, while Chameleon stashes them unwashed under the bed. Mender needs a predictable, orderly world. Chameleon eats chaos for every meal. Looks impossible, doesn't it?

The only way it can work is if Mender and Chameleon understand each other at very basic levels. They must also give each other enough space to live their lives without constant comment.

Menders need to accept Chameleons' nervous, fickle and rebellious ways. Chameleons should understand that they can't command Mender to be more emotionally responsive. When they accept each other's natures, life could be rewarding. Well, maybe not wonderful, but okay. Mender and Chameleon are too different to make each other completely happy.

Friends

This would be like Jacqueline Kennedy Onassis (who actually is a Mender) and Tiny Tim becoming best friends.

Siblings

Mommy takes Mender and Chameleon to a birthday party. Within an hour Chameleon has destroyed the decorations, climbed on the roof, ripped off a dozen shingles and swiped a couple of birthday presents. Meanwhile, Mender set all the plastic forks and paper plates according to Vanderbilt etiquette and stuffed all the party favor bags.

As adults, they seem to have been born into two different families.

Teacher-Student

It doesn't matter which one is the teacher. Either way, they will become impatient with each other and it won't make for a good learning situation.

At Work

It's hard to imagine this combination at the same work site, let alone cooperating with each other. Mender wouldn't be able to depend on Chameleon to show up, and Chameleon would play practical jokes on Mender just for fun.

A Mender boss has the necessary patience to supervise a Chameleon, but would probably prefer to have a reliable employee. A Chameleon boss may take advantage of Mender good nature, so Mender needs to be careful not to be exploited.

13. Chameleon in Relationships

∽

CHAMELEON-CHAMELEON

In Love

Two Chameleons together make Indiana Jones' life look dull. They have an amazingly hectic life, to say the least. Their home might look like the "As-Is" section of the Salvation Army store, with fuzzy things growing in the refrigerator, underwear scattered under cushions and in kitchen drawers. One couple I know of sleep in a tent in someone's backyard. Another have lived in a used Winnebago for their entire married life.

But if this couple has nothing else, they have a good time. They may take jobs only long enough to raise the money to travel. Two of my Chameleon friends started an import/export business so they could have an excuse to keep changing the scenery.

In one way or another, Chameleons must deal with each other's flightiness and hypersensitivity. If they recognize the need for spiritual development, they might enjoy meditation or yoga. They occasionally join communes, but don't often stay.

It's important for them to be aware of potential pitfalls, though, if they want their relationship to work. For example, they're fickle by nature. They are also indecisive, rebellious and lacking in common sense. The best insurance for this relationship is a commitment to be honest from both Chameleons.

Life will be exciting for the children of Chameleons if their parents' relationship is stable. They will probably be encouraged to be creative. If their parents turn against each other, however, the children are apt to become rebellious. Children from two Chameleons could wind up either in Juvenile Hall or on full scholarships to Harvard.

Friends

These two are probably the only friends who will readily admit that they don't understand each other. And without false assumptions to get in the way of their truly knowing each other, they can start their relationship with a clean slate. The only danger is that they will encourage each other to participate in the more sensational and "risky" side of life, including possibly involvement with crime, drugs, orgies or general debauchery.

Siblings

If one of them doesn't get the other banished to military school by high school, they might be friends for life. Their rooms may look like disaster areas, as Chameleons are notorious for disorder. Don't bother them with trivial things like sitting still in restaurants, folding their T-shirts and upgrading their report cards. It's a losing battle.

Teacher-Student

What would one Chameleon be likely to teach another? How to make opium pipes or the perfect martini, possibly? You just won't find Chameleons teaching in traditional classrooms unless they're professionals who are guest lecturers.

At Work

Think this pair wouldn't ever get to work? Wrong! Some Chameleons are actually workaholics. They compensate for their emotional confusion by concentrating on their careers. Though they may feel incompetent, they usually "fake it till they make it."

Chameleons are fun at the office, too. At best, they are great comedians, and at worst they're good for memorable one-liners. Often irreverent, they will playfully poke fun at the boss, and overall, they're a great antidote for office boredom!

Chameleon bosses can be excellent because they can see things from all sides and make decisions based on a broad range of feelings and facts.

Part 3
You and
Your World

14. How You See Yourself: Shape

Does your writing look like a row of umbrellas—round "m's" and "n's?"

Is it very rounded, composed solely of curved lines?

Does it form little cups along the baseline?

Is it angular and notched—like dandelion leaves?

Or is it wispy—loosely curved—with vanishing connections—like an unravelling ball of yarn?

What shape is your handwriting? You might say your handwriting is merely curved, straight, or curved *and* straight and leave it at that.

But it gets more complicated when you consider how many varieties there are of straight and curved lines.

Look at the general appearance of your letters and the connections between them.

There are five basic shapes of handwriting: Garland, Rounded, Arcade, Angular and Thready. Each one reveals a different personality. By studying shapes, you'll be able to determine a person's public image.

Actually, you can probably guess the shape of someone's writing by what people say about them. For example, suppose people often say you're warm and affectionate: chances are you make Garland shapes. Or perhaps people complain that you find fault with them too often: then it's more likely that you're an Angular writer.

Here are examples of the five basic handwriting shapes:

Garland   **Rounded**

possible   *In reference*

Arcade

beginning 𝒟

Angular

forget how many
Also, my handwriting

Thready

please send up

GARLAND WRITING

that they can
their lives, and

Notice how Garland handwriting gently curves as it contacts the baseline. Looking at it, you may get a warm feeling. That's not surprising, because Garland writers tend to be gentle, soft and loving. If you find an angry and critical Garland writer, look for other signs in the handwriting—such as sharply pointed t-bars or "resentment strokes." Garlanders don't have an *overtly* aggressive bone in their bodies. When angry, they'll be indirect. It's not that they're hypocritical, but just that they have trouble expressing anger.

Garland shapes are concave scooped connections, and they reveal an affectionate and receptive nature. There's a passive, non-competitive core in the Garland nature. That's the good news. The bad news is that Garlanders can overindulge in their own emotions and become unbearably sorry for themselves when life doesn't run smoothly.

Being self-indulgent, Garlanders can go overboard with their vices:

Garland bookworms buy more books than their shelves can hold and their schedules permit them to read.

"Garland Gourmand" may be redundant.

Emotional Garlanders specialize in going to movies that are sure to make them cry. They may easily become addicted to romance novels.

Why are Garlanders self-indulgent? On the positive side, they enjoy being emotional. On the negative side, they feel empty inside when they avoid dealing with their problems. So they try to fill that emptiness with smoke, drink, food or compulsive spending. They become less self-indulgent when they begin to label their inexplicable, complex and intense feelings.

Garlanders seem to take the easiest, most convenient path when they face obstacles. Did you just say, "Who doesn't?" Arcade and

Angular writers don't. They snack on yesterday's problems for breakfast and tomorrow's problems for dinner.

Garlanders are more philosophic than aggressive problem-solvers. Isaac Asimov, Mary Martin and Frank Lloyd Wright, all Garlanders, have shared their philosophies of life to help us understand and accept ourselves better. Many handwriting analysts are Garlanders (or they adopt that style when they learn about this positive Garland characteristic).

If you're a Garlander, you already know of your sensitivity, and you certainly don't want to change your basic nature. To you, being detached and objective would be boring, so you cultivate the more exciting, sensitive, empathic side of your nature. You seem able to feel what others feel as if you were in their place. But remember that it's important for you to surround yourself with positive people and to separate your own feelings from everyone else's. If you're around negative people, you can easily pick up on their moods, like a walking seismograph, and begin to think negatively, too.

Being more passive than active, it's likely that your friends choose you more often than you choose them. You're the "pickee," and your friends probably value your compassion and kindness.

Most people write with Garlands, and while these paragraphs describe many of them fairly well, there are variations that require a little more explanation. The four basic Garland types are Shallow, Deep, Hanging and Loopy.

Shallow Garlands

handwriting analyzed

I loved what the ma

If you find shallow connections and letters with low-slung bottoms, and the general Garland description doesn't seem right, it's because this writing provides some exceptions to the Garland rule.

The shallow Garland shape is the easiest one to create. It takes almost no effort, and this symbolize these Garlanders' movements through life—effortless and a little lazy. They like to be in touch with many people, but their bonds aren't likely to develop deeply. That's because they move lightly through life, and they don't have time to spend on relationships that they think will not have a lot of reward in them. Have you ever heard, "Let's do lunch," knowing there'd never be one?

These Garlanders have an urgent need to be noticed. If they couldn't be seen or heard, they'd shrivel up like a pepperoni on the bottom of a pizza oven. In attempts to be close, they're likely to be overly affectionate. They love having center stage, and sometimes they'd upstage their own mothers to get it—especially their own mothers.

They tend to be seductive, believing that charm can make up for almost anything. So they charm everyone, even those they'd like to strangle. If these writers would simply ask for what they want, their lives wouldn't become so complicated, and they'd find more fulfillment and less conflict in emotional matters.

These Garlanders do understand that they need more intimacy in their lives. All they have to do to get it is spend more time with people and recognize that no one is expendable. Then their emotional ties with others will strengthen.

P.S. Hugh Hefner has this Garland writing.

Deep Garlands

Well, here it is. I had to not to wait any longer— I don't know exactly what

These letters and connections look a bit like ladles, don't they?

If you find these shapes in the Garland handwriting, you'll find Garlanders who are extremely sensual and sentimental. Intensely emotional, they cherish all those sentiments the Hallmark greeting card company likes to express. Every corsage, every snapshot and every baby bootie that has ever touched their lives is pressed in a dictionary, tucked in a drawer or stashed in an old trunk. They host perfect parties, set perfect tables and memorize Amy Vanderbilt etiquette books, but they also connect deeply with others. To feel happy and complete they must have romance in their lives.

Hanging Garlands

This common handwriting trait—connections that sag below the baseline—indicates a fear of being taken advantage of. These writers have the basic, kind Garland nature, but they find it almost impossible to say "no." Therefore, they're often taken for granted and actually are frequently exploited.

They find emotional security in saving mementos and are likely to keep their Teddy Bears and "blankies" forever. (Could Steve "Hanging Garland" McQueen have slept with a stuffed animal? Maybe not, but he was known to be a recluse. Perhaps he felt the need to protect himself.)

These writers are often manipulated when they don't communicate what they want and take steps to get it. If they don't make responsible choices for themselves, others tend to take over and make career, marriage and friendship decisions for them. Then these Garlanders feel abused, bullied and angry.

Loopy Writing

know if there's anything
Thank you for your help

In order to call writing "loopy," it must have huge loops above and below the baseline. Generally, loopy writing means the writers are highly emotional. In fact, they're emotional junkies. They don't want to steal even a smidgeon of spontaneity from the emotional moment. Santa Anita installed guard rails just to keep these guys off the track.

Sensitive and hyper-responsive, they get exhausted easily. They usually have many changes going on in their lives. If they don't, they get restless. And although they leap before looking—and get into trouble because of it—they bounce back quickly from traumas, as loopy writer U.S. Senator Wilbur Mills did with his famous alcoholism recovery.

ROUNDED WRITING

My name is Katy D. The
'D" stands for Diane. I
may use that name, and
I might not. What do you
Think I should do?

Children usually create round letters with roundish connections. And it follows that adults who write this way project an innocent, naive image to the world. Many Rounded writers do seem to act immature and lack a sense of responsibility. Actually, they see themselves as their primary responsibility—and usually don't want to take care of anyone else.

Because Roundeds direct their attention to their inner needs and outer appearances, they excel at volunteer work. The next time you're visiting the hospital, notice the way the Candy Stripers sign their name tags, and you'll see what I mean. If you have teenage Roundeds at home, urge them to get involved with charity work. The praise they'll get for doing simple tasks is really what they want at this stage of their lives. Rounded writing is usually a passing phase.

But for some it's not. Sally Rand, the fan dancer, was a Rounded writer. Phyllis Diller is one. So is mass murderer, Richard Speck.

ARCADE WRITING

Arcade writing is difficult to recognize. Look for umbrella-like handwriting structures. Lower case "m" and "n" tops will be rounded, curved over—as in the example above. If "m's" and "n's" aren't rounded, but the writing doesn't fit into any other category, look for the following:

Direct connection from the lower to the upper zone

Umbrella "r"

Hooked-over "t's"

Arched, broad, sweeping, convex curves forming upper case letters, as in the "t" example above, is typical of arcade writing.

Arcades indicate the need for structure and protection—psychological as well as physical. Imagine a turtle. Compare the Arcade to a turtle shell. Turtles need a protective, hard shell and their shells are convex. From the outside, turtles look pretty tough. But without their shells, they're very fragile.

Arcaders seem to require psychological protection and get it by wearing a shell of privacy. Surprisingly, however—and in spite of this—they want to be leaders and set standards for others.

When only the "m's" and "n's" are arcade, Arcaders tend to be meticulous, methodical problem solvers. They are not usually fast learners, but they're thorough. They try to consider all the angles and fit together every clue until they come up with an ingenious solution to major problems. If they're wrong, it's often because they veered off on a tangent and tried to reinvent the wheel.

The arcade writer is concerned with physical, commonsense things. For example, Arcaders are likely to have an earthy sense of humor that is by no means subtle or difficult to understand. And if you ask them to deal with something abstract, they might not know what you're talking about unless you spell it out in steps: 1, 2 and 3.

Practical folk, Arcaders prefer to stay away from fanatics and fanatical thinking. They accept what they can see and feel and aren't big fans of "blind faith." They generally make the most of their potentialities and work within their limitations. Traditional ways of doing things make sense to them, because traditions have worked for so long.

Arcaders tend to resist major changes and may crumble under pressure. They aren't famous for flexibility or compromise. In fact, they're probably the most stubborn and conservative of all the writing shapes. But they do have admirable qualities of thrift and economy. They cope with, and perhaps enjoy, mundane chores, from weeding the garden to stuffing envelopes.

Sometimes they seem unaware of their emotional natures. But that's only because they find tangible things easier to deal with than emotions. Accustomed to ignoring their feelings, they're not always able to cope with emotional crises when they arise.

Dr. George Bach, the psychologist who wrote *Creative Aggression*, writes heavily with arcades.

Arcaders excel at creating efficient workplaces. But unless you remind them to include light, living things—like plants—they're apt to end up working in a drab brown cubby hole without a sign of life.

What do George McGovern, Pierre Trudeau, Gerry Ford, Jimmy Carter and Ronald Reagan all have in common? They are all Arcaders.

Heavily Arcaded Writing

Drug Abuse is a multi-faced dem Draining our resources, threatening ou and spreading itself a la an aids

These writers differ from general Arcaders in that they make life more complicated and dramatic than necessary. And in the process of complicating things, they may miss out on opportunities. For example, let's say there's a job opening at Widget Corporation, and Mr. Heavy Arcade wants a job. He spends days in the library, studies Widget in the *Standard and Poore Index*, sends for the Widget annual report, hangs out in Widget's cafeteria. When he gathers enough information, he applies for the job. It was filled three weeks before.

Extremely Arcaded

the Santa Monica know. I'm doing a place. It's opening

These Arcaders are more dynamic, dramatic and complicated than the Heavy Arcaders. They make strong and lasting impressions, and if they aren't in a position to be seen, they are apt to disappear from the scene altogether. They know that you never get a second chance to make a first impression—so they do it with great pizazz.

Are you surprised that Gloria Vanderbilt and Jacqueline Onassis do extremely arcaded writing?

Slinky Arcades

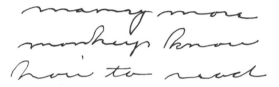

This writing seems to slink along the line. Remember that arcades *must be illegible* to be evaluated as Slinky. These Arcaders cloud issues and do not present facts in a plain and simple way. Positively said, these Arcaders have the power to make insecure people feel good about themselves. Negatively said, these writers are manipulative.

L. Ron Hubbard, Scientology mastermind, has a slinky arcade signature. Ronald Reagan's borders on slinkiness.

Tight Arcaders

Notice the retracing, or total lack of space between the "m" and "n" humps in the above example. This is a sign that Tight Arcaders are blind to their own emotional needs. They repress them, and after a while they are likely to become depressed. Tight Arcaders deserve to be happier and feel more secure than they do. And because they feel so emotionally threatened, they don't often have the energy to be outgoing and helpful.

Tight Arcaders seem to believe that if anyone really knew them, they wouldn't like them. What's actually going on? They think no one really wants to know them. Out of fear that they'll be misunderstood, they are reluctant to share their feelings. Therefore, their relationships don't reach the emotional depth that Garlanders are able to achieve.

Mary Tyler Moore is a Tight Arcader.

ANGULAR WRITING

writing this note to give you something evaluate. So what can you tell me I don't already know?

Angular writing often lacks loops and has very sharp connections to the baseline. Look for pointed tops on "m," "n" and sometimes "h" humps. If the "l" loops are narrow and pointy, too, you've got an Angular writer.

Angulars are ruled by ever-active, adrenalin-producing emotions, such as anger, rage and intense glee. They are the least likely of all these types to cope effectively with sadness, depression or any kind of feeling that requires contemplation to get through in one calm piece.

They are often intensely passionate, but only when *they* want to be. And they don't always express their love with great sensitivity. For example, when Angulars feel frisky, it doesn't matter what their lovers are busy with—no matter how important—they seldom take "no" for answer.

Angulars are usually extroverted, positive and ACTIVE. Garlanders may get annoyed with them for not being good listeners, but Angulars have so much energy they aren't always able to control it.

What's the bottom line? (Angulars love the phrase "bottom line.") Their goal in life is to be P-E-R-F-E-C-T. They may even think they've attained perfection, so they get very upset when they blunder. Or they deny that they commit errors at all.

Angulars see the world in terms of black and white, right or wrong. Nothing is neutral. Many proclaim that there are two kinds of people, "achievers and bums." And even though they don't readily admit to having weaknesses, they're quick to point out weaknesses in others—especially when they have the same flaws.

In response to sadness, Angulars typically make jokes about their own unhappiness. And since they don't let go and really express their emotions themselves, they try to make other people "cheer up," too. Angular usually doesn't understand that the other person (let's say, a Garlander), actually wants to cry it out. Then Angular becomes indignant: "Well, I just wanted to help!" Angulars need to develop more empathy.

It must be said, however, that Angulars don't demand more of others than they do of themselves—even though they demand a lot. As they learn to be less judgmental, they may be able to accept the fact they too have faults.

It must have been an Angular who said, "I was only wrong one time in my life and that's when I thought I was wrong, but I was really right."

Angulars need, want and would like to get *immediate results* for their efforts. They work long hours, often forgetting to eat because they're so work-oriented. If their t-bars are strong and long, they will only work with others who give up lunch hours, too. Does that mean they're impatient and sometimes unreasonable? Yes.

They love a challenge. In fact, they're sometimes thought of as trouble-makers because they tend to challenge everything and everyone. Discriminating people, they operate on the unspoken rule: "Whatever Is Popular, I'm Against." That's not to insult Angulars—it's their point of pride to protest and have their own opinions.

Don't think that they're impossible to please and too fussy. They just need to be won over to your point of view.

Angulars are the daring people among us, and their plans and ideas—if tempered by Garlands—will ultimately change the world. But remember that Angulars often become disappointed and disillusioned. In their need to change and challenge existing circumstances, they don't acknowledge obstacles, delays and intermittent failures.

When Angulars learn to calculate their risks, start new projects cautiously, and realize that it's okay that some things go wrong, and that some people oppose them, they will experience less disappointment.

Angulars have a fiery spirit. They break through restrictions and melt down opposition. They have a burning desire to take control and may get pushy, because they believe that opportunities come only to those who seize them. Napoleon Bonaparte and Robert E. Lee were both Angulars.

Angulars have a dramatic, intense quality. When forced to wait for others, they get anxious, as if they'll stagnate forever if things don't keep moving all the time. As a result of that frustration, they sometimes forge ahead without careful planning, seeking action for action's sake. If you want to torture Angulars, show up late for a date, drive in the slow lane, speak slowly and put them on "hold."

Nazi Gestapo chief Heinrich Himmler and the famous lover Giovanni Casanova were both Angulars. And just think how different psychoanalysis would be today if Dr. Sigmund Freud wasn't one, too.

THREADY WRITING

Right now my business is going through a weary period. It has caused me to consider taking a full-time job in changing fields.

If you squint at this writing, it looks as though the wind is blowing it in loose threads across the page. Like the wind, a Thready is unpredictable and lacks traditional discipline.

Have you wondered why your Thready friend has not yet built that better mousetrap? Undoubtedly, because it's not the right time. Threadies have their own conception of time and space and move to the beat of their own tamborine.

These writers are sensitive to their own feelings and don't normally pay much attention to other people's feelings. But remember that this writing shape indicates profound creativity. You're dealing with an artistic type and artistic temperament. They're influenced by ideas that they can't explain. They're inspired (sometimes brilliantly), but won't be able to explain how they got inspired. They don't know. Andy Warhol was a Thready.

Socially, they rebel against traditional ways of doing things, not as Angular goes against the grain, but in subtle, less blatant ways. If they want to be more effective in communicating their ideas and more successful, they may need to pay more attention to public opinion or develop their enormous sensitivity further by learning how to listen.

If Thready writing floats above the baseline, the writer probably thinks in abstractions. Threadies are usually above average in intelligence, the people most likely to help transcend our planetary limitations.

Threadies are logical, and their concerns are usually centered around mass consciousness raising, rather than limited to one or two people. Amelia Earhart, Booker T. Washington and Balzac were all Threadies.

Although Threadies are more sociable than Angulars, they're not extremely close to their friends. If fact, their friends are usually little more than acquaintances. That's because they want to know as many people as possible. They want to comprehend the whole world—not just a few people. In highly-charged emotional relationships, the bond itself might cloud their perceptions of life. So getting intensely involved with only one person could interfere with their experiencing the whole world. This is an important point, because many Threadies think that they're here to do Everything. That's a lot of ground to cover.

If clear, logical thinking and breadth of vision is Threadies' great strength, then the inability to get emotionally involved is their weakness. This weakness can be aggravated if they don't see a lack of sensitivity on their part as part of the problem. They need to develop insight into human nature to match their profound comprehension of life.

15. Compatibilities of Letter Shapes and Connections

Generally, each writer gets along best with the same type of shape-maker. They understand each other fairly easily. If two people don't share the same writing shape at the beginning, there's a chance their writing shapes will begin to look alike after a while.

If the person whose writing you're studying doesn't write with even a smattering of your shape of handwriting, it may seem that you're from two different universes. You are. If you stay together, you'll need to appreciate that fact!

GARLANDERS-GARLANDERS

Having this writing shape in common is a big, potential plus. Both are emotionally receptive people who can relate to each other without competing. Their strongest advantage is that they each want to be accepted by the other. Finding conflict intolerable, they will probably do everything they can to make things comfortable.

At the movies they'll have contests as to who can scream the loudest or go through the most tissues.

GARLANDERS-ROUNDEDS

Garlanders inevitably feel that it's their job to take care of Roundeds. It's as if the Garlanders are the mothers and the Roundeds are the teenagers. In any sort of relationship, the

Garlanders may get tired of doing all the work and want their needs met in return. Because Roundeds haven't emotionally bloomed yet, they are probably not going to be as sensitive to others' needs as they will be in the future. If they mature, they may be only as sensitive as they have to be to keep the relationship going.

In a love relationship, Roundeds are basically like Garlanders, but they may not be able to see things from Garlanders' perspective. To make the relationship satisfying for both, they should have a rich and varied social life, and an emotionally supportive extended family. (It won't hurt, either, for them to have enough money to have fun!)

GARLANDERS-ARCADERS

As Garland writing is composed of concave, cuplike curves, Arcade is convex, umbrellalike. That illustrates the complementary attraction between Garlanders and Arcaders.

Garlanders are emotional. Arcaders are protective. If the Garlanders express creativity, and the Arcaders uphold tradition with great authority, the relationship can be an excellent one. Peace will prevail, as long as the Garlanders respect the fact that Arcaders don't like fast changes or challenges to their ways of life. The Arcaders need to understand that Garlanders need plenty of approval, attention and affection—and provide it.

GARLANDERS-ANGULARS

Garlanders and Angulars may complement each other, but it's not likely. They will achieve harmony if the Garlanders don't assert themselves *ever*, and if the Angulars won't be overly judgmental, critical and perfectionistic. That might prove to be more than they each want to handle. This holds true for all kinds of relationships, and it will take quite a lot of work for a friendship to survive the strain these two would put on it.

Garlanders easily use Angulars as excuses for not actively pursuing their goals. "If it weren't for you, I'd be a star by now," says

Garlander. The truth is Garlander would rather complain than actually do anything about becoming a star. Angulars readily take the blame for overwhelming and dominating Garlanders, because Angulars are accustomed to being accused of being domineering.

GARLANDERS-THREADIES

In any kind of relationship Garlanders and Threadies can get along well because they enjoy active social lives. They could, however, manage to cut off real communication between them by keeping busy every time they get together. Their friendship could become one of those fun, non-serious, no-questions-asked relationships everyone seems to need.

Romantically, everything should go fine until the Garlanders need more approval and more attention than they are able to extract from Threadies. In family life, the Garlanders may turn to the children as their only source of emotional satisfaction. That might work— until the children grow up and move away from home. Then the Garlanders' new demands on their Thready mates may prove disastrous, unless both partners consciously reassess their relationship.

ROUNDEDS-ROUNDEDS

Whether the relationship be working or loving or friendly, two Roundeds together are all fun and probably no seriousness. Roundeds need more attention and nurturing than another Rounded is willing to give. In addition, Roundeds by definition are at best childlike and at worst childish. So a longterm relationship between them is not likely to develop without some severe emotional crisis that forces them to mature.

ROUNDEDS-ARCADERS

Arcaders generally have little patience with Roundeds' emotionalism. And the Arcade authoritarianism and traditionalism is a turnoff to the Roundeds. They should have other things in common, such as slant, zone emphasis or high t-bars for their friendship to succeed.

ROUNDEDS-ANGULARS

Roundeds may feel threatened by Angular assertiveness and perfectionism. Rounded innocence may be fascinating in the beginning, but in the long run, Angular won't appreciate having to protect Roundeds from the real world. Roundeds are usually too idealistic, dreamy and impractical for the no-nonsense Angular to want to put up with for long.

ROUNDEDS-THREADIES

Roundeds want to play all day. So do Threadies. If they played Monopoly, Roundeds would be stuck with one or two low-rent properties while Threadies would end the game owning hotels on Boardwalk and Park Place, all the railroads and utilities, and they'd probably find a way to own Jail and take a commission on passing Go. The way each one plays Monopoly will give you a good idea of the way they live. Roundeds are passive bystanders in life. Threadies figure out how to work every aspect of the system to their advantage without ever having to fully join it. The extent to which they'd get along depends on how much compassion the Thready has for the Rounded.

ARCADERS-ARCADERS

For all kinds of relationships, this is a good combination because they respect each other's privacy and areas of *inflexibility*. That makes it difficult to have a passionately intense relationship, but they certainly understand one another. Arcaders are just as needy as Garlanders, but they know how to hide it.

Arcaders often release their emotions dramatically. The more wild and encompassing the arches in the handwriting, the more creative, imaginative and attention-seeking the writer. Eve Arden and Priscilla Presley are both Arcaders.

ARCADERS-ANGULARS

While Arcaders rely on their instincts, Angulars act only upon reason. Both types tend to be inflexible and unyielding people who will compromise only at gunpoint. If they share the same address, they should have separate rooms at opposite ends of the house.

If they're pondering marriage, they should make sure that they have identical values, goals and the same level of passion. Then if they equally divide the workload, it might work. But if they aren't in basic agreement on childraising techniques and what they want out of life, they're inviting problems.

Let's say they're buying a new family car. Angular will research every back issue of *Consumer Reports* and choose the one that proves to be the safest based on extensive crash-tests, and the best deal. Arcader would choose based solely on a quick start on cold mornings, and the quality of the stereo.

ARCADERS-THREADIES

In relationships Arcaders can provide financial security and structure, while Threadies provide an element of intrigue and surprise. This would seem a better combination for friendship or light romance than for business or marriage. But, of course, when you're talking about Threadies, you need to find out whether the Thready is hard to understand and evasive or sensitive and quick-thinking.

Arcaders in the kitchen go by the book (the cookbook) or they write their own. Threadies add ingredients you never thought of adding. Ever had a peanut butter salad dressing or grated lemon rinds in chili? Threadies do lots of things you'd never think of doing. One Thready I know bought a professional sno-cone maker and a cotton candy machine and installed them in a pinball gallery next to his pool and jacuzzi. His Arcader wife is in charge of inviting people over.

ANGULARS-ANGULARS

Angulars are perfectionistic, fault-finding and critical, but they're also high-energy, passionate, exuberant people. They fly off the handle about things that most other types would pass by without notice. For example, no Garlander would see the need for traffic lights inside grocery stores. Angulars do.

The problem with two Angulars together is that they're so goal-oriented, they might not take enough time to be together. If they're friends, they'll rarely find time to see one another (unless their meeting is business-related). If they're mates, they need to make dates with each other as if they're still wooing. But for the sake of their health, they should make those dates non-food related. Angulars don't eat; they practically gulp their food without chewing.

ANGULARS-THREADIES

At best Angulars make Threadies buckle down and get serious with ultimatums of suicide or murder. At worst the Angulars make Threadies buckle down and get serious with ultimatums of suicide or murder.

A perfect Sunday to Thready is to go to the beach to tan, to bodywatch, to admire the roller-skaters in action and to lie around with a tall glass of lemonade. That same Sunday would be a torment to an Angular, who would rather mow the lawn or get back to work.

I don't know any reason why these two would get together. If they have to relate because they work together or they're in the same family, a smart supervisor or parent would get them to realize that they're two thoroughly different people with different goals.

THREADIES-THREADIES

Two Threadies will either manipulate or delight each other—or both. It depends on the rest of the handwriting and the motives of the Threadies. They're usually difficult to figure out. As soon as you determine which pigeonhole to put them in, they're in another one. Because they're usually up to something, most Threadies are excruciatingly funny and entertaining. I know a dermatologist Thready who is known to his friends' children as David the Balloonman, because he bought a helium tank just to blow up their balloons. He also befriends world-famous chefs, learns their special skills and shares this calorie-laden talent with his friends. His Thready wife transformed the hall closet into a bathroom where they built a replica of a throne to be used for the toilet.

16. Life Focus: Zones

Which area of your life means the most to you? When spring arrives, and everyone outside your window is running, biking and roller skating, are you inside reading Dostoevski? Are you busy with your annual cleanup? Perhaps you don't know it's spring because you're deep in the vault counting your money. Or maybe you enjoy all these things come spring.

What we're looking at in this chapter is your life focus, and we get to it by examining the three zones of your handwriting:

UPPER ZONE:
The Future: Imagination, Ideas, Spirituality, Fantasy, Goals
Letters: b,d,f,h,k,l,t

MIDDLE ZONE:
The Here and Now: Daily routine, communication, reality, practicalities
Letters: a,c,e,m,n,o,r,s,u,v,w,x

LOWER ZONE:
The Past: Drives, Money, Memory, Sexual expression, Dreams, Unconsciousness
Letters: f,g,j,p,q,y,z

The handwriting zone you emphasize reflects that life focus. You can easiliy determine which zone is emphasized by measuring your handwriting with a metric ruler.

Average middle zone letters are 2 mm high
Average upper zone letters extend 5 mm above the baseline
Average lower zone letters extend 5 mm below the baseline
(There are 25.4 mm to an inch.)

The model handwriting has an upper zone and lower zone exactly 2.5 times higher and lower than the middle zone. For example, if your middle zone measures 2 mm high, your upper zone measures 5 mm high, and your lower zone measures 5 mm below the baseline, you have perfect handwriting zonal proportion.

Let's say your middle zone measures 3 mm high, your upper zone measures 5 mm high, and your lower zone measures *more than* 7.5 mm below the baseline, your writing would show lower zone dominance.

Here are a few examples of upper, middle and lower zone emphasis.

Over-developed upper zone

Over-developed middle zone

Over-developed lower zone

THE UPPER ZONE

Upper Zone Emphasis

Big upper loops, flourishing capital letters, super tall t-stems and pillowy d-loops are all indications that this person is probably intelligent and lives to read, pray, philosophize or dream. Under stress there will be an escape into fantasy life.

If you emphasize the upper zone, you focus on what-could-be and what-if, rather than what is. You might dream of a Zen garden, for example, but it's doubtful that you'll swing out of the hammock, grab a shovel and relandscape the yard.

Non-Loopers

We are thinking about going to th moving up north someplace — after

Because loops represent imagination and emotion, their absence reveals a practical nature. Non-loopers are objective and don't trust their instincts. This is your basic fact-gatherer. Non-loopers learn for the sake of learning. They make excellent researchers.

Wild-Loopers

not overly athletic fit. I thoroughly enjoy oldies and sundown

Wild-loopers have so many interests they can't keep track of them all. Their imaginations are so active that they sometimes have trouble separating fact from fantasy. The negative side of Wild-loopers is that the only access they have to their feelings is through fantasy, and they may seek ideal situations that don't exist. They also may feel that they deserve special treatment when they have done nothing to earn it.

Non-Looped Upper Zone

These practical writers retrace their upstrokes instead of creating loops. But the price they pay for being so accountable and dependable is their creative imagination. For example, they would rather write a paper based on carefully gathered data than on their own opinions. They'd certainly be more likely to write nonfiction than science fiction.

Pointed Upper Zone Loops

Where you see pointed upper loops, you may find lonely, isolated people who have a false sense of being different and better than those around them. If the pointed loop occurs on the personal pronoun "I," isolation is a major problem.

Lack of Upper Zone

These writers are confused about how they appear to other people, what they want out of life and where they're going. It's likely that they're also either agnostics or atheists. In any case, spirituality doesn't play a significant role in their lives.

THE MIDDLE ZONE

Middle Zone Emphasis

Putting an emphasis on the middle zone, where the small letters are written (e's, a's, w's, etc.) at the expense of making significant loops high or low, show the writer's self-reliance and practicality.

Huge Middle Zone

hand can write! By the way. love explanation marks!

These writers are primarily concerned with keeping house, keeping up and keeping busy. They're not particularly interested in religion or philosophy, and they often lack a healthy fantasy life. They'd rather read the Sunday funny pages, ride their bikes, or climb mountains than play chess or watch a documentary. In fact, one huge middle zoner I know claims that there is only one nature show, and PBS keeps playing it over and over.

Writers with huge middle zones hate, detest and abhor abstract notions. They want to know specifics and concrete definitions. For instance, they relate to "How-to" books that give step-by-step instructions. Most handwriting samples that I evaluate are middle zone dominant. It suggests to me that these writers are hungry to know more about themselves. They also want to know how to solve complex problems quickly and efficiently. The most important point about dominant middle zoners is that when they want something, they want it NOW. And they feel frustrated unless they get immediate gratification.

Squashed and Scrunched Middle Zone

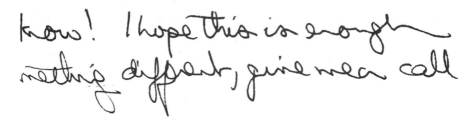

Closely spaced words mean the writers are repressing the need to expand their horizons. If the "e's" look like little slits and the "m's" are compressed, the situation is even worse. These people are stuck in ruts and are so busy tending to everyday details that they've forgotten how exciting life can be.

Microscopic Handwriting

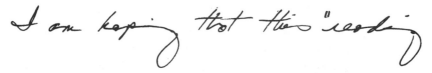

If you feel the urge to use your magnifying glass when you read it, you're looking at microscopic writing. It's usually middle zone dominant. The writer has tunnel-vision and achieves goals through persistence.

Underdeveloped Middle Zone

When there's hardly any middle zone emphasis or any height at all to the small letters, take a closer look: these writers may be geniuses or great con artists. They're able to block out all their ego needs as they concentrate intensely. They may be the computer Whiz

Kids of Silicon Valley who will eventually revolutionize the world by inventing new approaches to old problems. High intelligence isn't always associated with this trait, but it is often enough for us to take the time to analyze it further.

Uneven Middle Zone Height

yet. (Hopefully, by the time I will be present an adequate represen

The uneven middle zone writer is very moody, and the root of the problem might be found in a chronic blood or hormone disorder. Regardless of the cause, this person doesn't cope well with daily ups and downs. If you find that the lower case "i's" are very tiny, the writer has a weak self-image.

THE LOWER ZONE

Huge Lower Zone

you. This is an ongoing process

Writing that's dominated by huge lower loops is an indication that the writer is restless, driven and often confused. Huge lower loops usually tangle into the lines below them. If the lines aren't tangled together with long, roundish loops, as in the above example, it means the writers evade problems rather than confront them directly.

But huge lower loops always indicate that the writers urgently want things to change in their lives. They usually believe that money or a new relationship will make all the difference to their lives.

Tangled Lower Loops

To create ways of being in par hip with staff, with patien with the community that I

With tangled lines, the writer is confused, uncertain as to which biological or emotion need to satisfy first. "Am I hungry? Tired? Do I want company? Maybe I should call Susan? No, I think I'll go for a drive . . . ."

This is usually a temporary handwriting characteristic. But when chronic, these writers have trouble separating work life from family life from social life.

Long Strokes Down Under

I enjoy working with my nephew.

Short or long ink trails that travel below the baseline without returning indicate people who are overly sensitive and fearful that their vulnerabilities will be exposed and taken advantage of. They often think they're being exploited and may be unlikely or unable to commit to a permanent relationship. If the person you love writes like this, a great deal of reassurance from you may be needed. See Chapter 19 for all the lower loop varieties.

BALANCED ZONES

*A tried for a free flow
I'm not sure I believe*

This example shows balanced zones and reflects a rounded personality. These people efficiently manage and structure their time, energy and living spaces. They're the ones who invented time management and goal planning.

ZONE COMPATIBILITY

Generally speaking, people who share the same zone emphasis will be more compatible with each other than those who don't, more likely to share goals and activities. But then, many workable combinations are possible, too. For example, a football fan will probably have a large lower zone. Would an upper zone dominant spouse who likes to spend Sundays reading or listening to music be sympatico? It's not likely, but compromise is possible. And isn't that what it's all about—flexibility and compromise? Maybe, maybe not. But now at least you're armed with more information for The Compatibility Test on page 196.

17. BRAIN POWER

Do you come up with the punchline during the setup of a joke? Do you feel double-crossed by crossword puzzles, because you never remember the four-letter name for the Baltic feeder? Some people solve problems slowly, some quickly, and some would rather shovel snow out of ten driveways than solve any kind of brainteaser.

The workings of the mind in the process of solving problems and making decisions are multi-faceted. It is quite fascinating to learn how others demonstrate the elusive concept of intelligence.

Most people have one major way to activate their grey cells, but some of us use a whole array. In this chapter we'll be looking at the qualities associated with intelligence—qualities that dramatize the different ways we think and solve problems.

Can we actually estimate intelligence from handwriting? Yes, graphologists have developed a technique that determines IQ within five points of a standardized test such as the Stanford Binet. It's a complicated, advanced procedure, and we won't go that far in this book. In any case, the basic handwriting characteristics that reveal intelligence and mental processing are easy to learn. These will reveal the different ways we mentally attack problems. For example, the differences between "m's" and "n's" will tell us about creative versus investigative mental processing. Connectedness between letters will tell us about systematic, persistent and realistic thinking versus intuitive, feeling-oriented thinking.

You can use this information on brain power the next time you're considering who deserves your vote in a national election. Or you might select an attorney, doctor or teacher based on handwriting, too.

THE M'S AND N'S

Sharp Writing

may need

Most of these letters have sharp tops and jabs at the baseline *within* the "m's" and "n's". The sharper the letters, the more quickly the person's mind works. How sharp is the writer? He's so sharp, he can actually walk like Sherlock Holmes into a room of strangers, size up the situation, know who's doing what to whom, and proceed directly to where he'll fit in the best.

If this is your writing, you may be so impulsive that you leap into action without gathering enough facts. You probably reach conclusions faster than a computer beep. If you speak your mind, you're true to form, and you join the good company of Robert Frost, Barry Goldwater, Carol Burnett and Tiny Tim. You prefer working alone (if lower loops aren't full), thinking logically and reflecting on new ideas. You need daily challenges in order to feel productive, and crave immediate results.

Rounded and Expanding M's and N's

administrative

Notice how the tops of the "m's" and "n's" are rounded, but how the strokes form little v's at the baseline. These people are adept at making new contacts and favorable impressions, at verbalizing articulately, generating enthusiasm and creating a motivating environment. They can be very entertaining.

In time, they can take a monumental problem, break it into bite-sized components and arrive at a practical solution. Sound like the method Thomas Edison used when he invented the light bulb and a couple of other things? He was this kind of writer.

If this is your writing, you have great potential, but you could benefit from cultivating greater objectivity, emotional control and a sense of urgency. You're idealistic, and that's not bad, but others may see you as a pussy cat because you're not particularly firm or definite in your dealings with them. If you want to be seen that way—fine. But if you want to be more assertive, notice when your relaxed attitude works against your goals.

Rounded and Compressed M's and N's

Rounded "m's" and "n's" ("h's," too) reveal writers who carefully collect twice as much information as the sharp writers do. They "manufacture" answers slowly and painstakingly rather than jump to conclusions.

If this is your writing, you think carefully, but sometimes you may be accused of being tedious. That's not to say you're not intelligent: you're just more methodical than most people. You "snowball" data. You build fact upon fact until you need no more. Then you are ultra-creative in your solutions.

To advance at a faster pace at work, you need to develop more authority than you have right now and stronger leadership skills. You need to delegate more tasks to others, spend less time on insignificant details and be less stubborn when faced with opposition.

In order to secure your place at work, you often establish sensible, conservative ways of doing things. When you feel appreciated, and your authority is accepted within the work group, you snuggle comfortably and contentedly into the cozy niche you've created for yourself. Doesn't that sound like Mary on the *Mary Tyler Moore Show?* Maybe she wasn't acting, because her real life signature shows two very compressed M's.

LOGIC & CONNECTEDNESS

Connected Writing

When a large number of letters are connected within a word, the writers are able to link one thought to another without interrupting their internal dialogue. They seldom hesitate when they speak, and they're determined and realistic. (Though you stop to dot an "i" or cross a "t," you're still considered a connected writer.)

These people are extremely logical. Compulsively logical. They rapidly follow a thought from beginning to end. Don't argue with them if your writing is disconnected. You'll never win, and you'll feel like a fool for trying.

However, they tend to get bogged down, because they have a compulsive need to be right all the time. They sometimes don't see the writing for the t-bars—meaning they fret over little, insignificant details. And because they're so quick in their thinking, they may offer advice when no one wants it. If this is you and you're tired of hearing, "Who asked you?" you might start becoming aware of circumstances in which you could be more diplomatic. Everyone knows you're bright. You don't have to advertise it.

Napoleon had such connected writing that he often attached

words to each other. We all know he felt he had to prove himself. They even named a "complex" for him.

Please don't think that connected writing is negative. Abraham Lincoln often wrote this way, too.

Partially Disconnected Writing

Limited opportunities at

People who create a few breaks here and there within a word are similar in their thinking to the totally connected writer. Their thoughts follow logically, but they aren't avid sticklers for detail. They're more broad-minded and less compulsive about being right and perfect all the time. Henry Miller, the Marquis de Sade and Robert Frost all exhibit this writing style.

Totally Disconnected Writing

definition of leaning is when I'm alone, I don't

Here the sense of logic is interrupted so that new ideas can come in. It is almost impossible for these writers to finish a thought without interrupting themselves. Many people won't consider it a compliment if you tell them they have disconnected thinking patterns. However, tell them that Michelangelo and Nietzsche both wrote that way, and they'll be correct in concluding that disconnected writing also indicates creativity and inspirational thinking.

When disconnected writers ask you what it means to insert many breaks within a word, you could say it means their ideas come from their emotions rather than reason. Or you could say it shows intuition. And you won't be wrong, because this writing is often associated with anticipating the needs of other people in an almost psychic way.

This is not to say that professional psychics disconnect their letters. In fact, many psychics connect all letters within words. Disconnected writing indicates that you have an intuitive way of knowing what other people want. It may also mean that you're *too* sensitive to everyone's feelings. You absorb what other people are feeling, and then think that what you're experiencing is coming from yourself. This sensitivity makes it uncomfortable for you to be with large groups of people. Haven't you ever wondered why you prefer aisle seats at the theater and the first or last row seats in a classroom?

Slow Writing

Thank you for your attention. If you have any questions

Slow writing is generally large, loopy and over-embellished. You get the feeling that these writers took a lot of time and care forming each letter. They don't react and think quickly. If this is your writing—and you want to be more effective—you need to develop short-cuts. You tend to waste time on irrelevant details. Perhaps that's because you don't think you can rely upon yourself alone. It's true that we all need other people, but that need is overdeveloped in you, and it's not working to your advantage.

Joan Crawford, Walt Disney and mass murderer, Richard Speck all wrote slowly.

Fast Writing

Lately it's getting more & more
—some letters are dropping out

This writing looks smooth and simple, and there's a spontaneity to it. Fast writers have natural efficiency and seem to know how to set complicated situations straight in a matter of moments. They are imaginative, and if the writing is legible, it's a sign of soaring intelligence—as exhibited in the writing of Amelia Earhart, Richard Nixon and L. Ron Hubbard.

Average Speed Writing

I am in the midot of a perform

This writing falls between fast and slow. Each stroke looks simple, but the large loops indicate that the writer took more time than a fast writer would. It shows average thinking speed.

FACTORS THAT ENHANCE INTELLIGENCE

Sense of Humor

m

n

The "smiles" on "m's" and "n's" represent a sense of humor. No joke. Humor occurs when the "unrelated" somehow outrageously relates. To be able to detect relationships where none should exist is a sign of intelligence.

Concentration

If you're a microscopic handwriter, you're a Tunnel Visionist, and nothing stands in the way of your getting what you want. That means your ability to focus on a goal surpasses that of most other writers. That intense focus is concentration at its best.

Independent Thinking

wanted

Short "t" and "d" stem writers are drop-outs from the school of conformism. If you make short "t's" and "d's", you'd make a terrible Rajneeshi, a hopeless Republican and you wouldn't be caught dead in designer clothes.

Attention to Details

in

A careful i-dotter attends to details. The desire to get things right certainly helps to put intelligence to work.

Directness

deal with

pretty things

No beating around the bush here. Elimination of introductory strokes means the writer takes the shortest distance between thought and expression. If this is you, and someone asks you what you think, you'll tell them, all right! No cat's got your tongue.

Flexibility

flights

This sample sings, "I Got Rhythm," because it's graceful, its "s's" are rounded and the "g's" and "f's" are figure eights. That gentle flow indicates flexibility—and flexible attitudes are important to intelligence.

Good Memory

altogether

The harder the pen presses the paper, the better the writer's memory and the greater the intelligence.

FACTORS THAT DETRACT FROM INTELLIGENCE

Absent-mindedness

interest

Carelessly placed i-dots and t-bars indicate you lose your glasses, forget your birthday and probably roam around for hours in underground parking lots searching for your car. Does that make you less intelligent? Maybe not, but it certainly impairs your efficiency when you lock yourself out of your office.

Indecisiveness

about exactly

Faded t-bars and aborted word endings point towards indecision. This trait paralyzes decisionmaking and forces the writer to depend on others for advice and direction.

Impulsiveness

impulsive

The far right (Reactor) slant points to supreme impulsiveness, suggesting that Reactors don't take enough time to gather the facts before arriving at a conclusion.

Part 4
You In Relationships

18. Relating to Others: Spacing

Communication is contact. People say, "I was really *touched* by what you said." Without verbal or written contact, most people feel isolated and depressed. Communication has been a popular topic for the last dozen years or so—the dire need for it to make groups and families function, to reconcile couples' differences and to raise children. And no matter how we feel about the importance of open communication, we have to give it more than lip service. Here we'll take a look at the different communication styles we adopt to talk to ourselves and to others and how they are reflected in handwriting.

Communication style is revealed by the use of space: the amount of space in oval vowel closings, between letters, words and lines. When we get to specific word and letter spacings, we'll take a look at how they are affected by slant, as well.

DEGREES OF EXPRESSIVENESS

How free are we to express our feelings? To find out, examine the formations of the "a" and the "o." It helps to think of these letters as little mouths. Are they open wide, slightly open, tightly sealed? Are there loops on one side or the other (or both)? Some handwriting will reveal a wide range of vowel formations, but usually one type will predominate. I call the communicators Chatterbox, Open, Reluctant, Should-doers, Secretive, Evasive and Explosive.

Chatterbox

Wide open vowels make you think of a wide open mouth, of course, and you won't be far off. This mouth is wide open because Chatterboxes can't be restrained, and they scatter their energy, talking constantly. You'll never have to wonder what Chatterboxes are feeling, because you'll get minute-to-minute reports. If you think your phone bill is ridiculous, look at theirs!

Chatterbox is often preoccupied with other sorts of oral activity as well, such as smoking, eating, chewing, nail-biting, spitting and thumbsucking.

If you're a Chatterbox, you may fear that silence reveals more than speech. And you feel that if you keep talking long enough and fast enough, no one will have a chance to see the real you between your lines. You may be trying to hide the fact that you feel socially insecure. But by talking incessantly, you deny yourself the opportunity to connect with others, because your chatter keeps them at a distance. In the long run that will make you feel even more awkward.

One major problem may be that you're inclined to exaggerate your own feelings. For example, if you fight with a friend, you'll chew on it until your hurt feelings get blown out of proportion. You'll find yourself getting more and more furious, and you may never be able to reconnect with your friend

The openness of the vowels isn't only like a mouth. It's also an openness to what people tell you. It may be useful to take the time to think things through before you speak and before you believe. If you find yourself complaining that others aren't taking you seriously, perhaps you'd benefit from selecting your words more carefully to get your points across more economically. Although, many Chatterboxes get points across quite well—Fidel Castro, for example!

Open

I could write more if you want

Small openings—seemingly insignificant ones within oval letters— show an ideal communication style. These small openings tell you that the writer discusses feelings appropriately, discreetly and economically.

If you're an Open, you take others people's feelings into account (depending on slant and shape, of course), but you're not above swapping a little gossip now and then. With your gift for natural conversational give and take, you make others feel right at home.

The Great American Novel, *Moby Dick,* was written by Open Herman Melville.

Reluctant

before I think cant anymore. I just wasnt had stuff to let go of int needed to know firsthand

Reluctants' ovals are tightly shut, reflecting an unwillingness to discuss feelings. In fact, this writer's feelings may be something of a mystery. Reluctants appear as strong, silent types. They create a romantic challenge to Opens and Chatterboxes, because there's a subtle air of seduction in that reserve.

If you're a Reluctant, it doesn't mean you don't like to talk. It's just that you don't like to discuss your feelings until you thoroughly trust the other person. You're either uncomfortable with feelings— unable to define them—or you believe your feelings are no one's business. You're very trustworthy with secrets.

Ted Kennedy, Gerald Ford, Tom Bradley and George Wallace all know how to keep their vowels shut. FDR didn't.

Should-Doers

She has all the credentials office person. Will our person blend? Can she collect more nice to people?

Should-Doers fill ovals with left loops and live a life of self-perpetuating guilt. Why "Should-Doers?" Because they begin so many sentences with "I should." They soothe guilty feelings by convincing themselves that it's their obligation to solve everyone's problems.

For instance, Should-Doer says, "I should feed all the neighbors' pets when they're away (even though I don't have time), because I'm a good person."

If you're a Should-Doer, you convince yourself your true feelings and desires don't count. Why? Because if you truly did what you wanted, and didn't do what everyone else wanted, you might have to admit you aren't a perfect person all the time. Your outer and inner images are at stake when you say no. So you're terminally nice.

Consider this typical Should-Doer scenario:

One day Should-Doer stays in bed with the flu. Her sister-in-law calls and asks Should-Doer to sew for her. Does Should-Doer say she's too sick? No way. She gets up, pulls out the sewing machine and runs off two sets of curtains and a bedspread.

Should-Doer believes she's a caring and giving person. She would feel terrible about committing an insensitive act. Not helping would mean to her that she didn't care. What makes her situation even more pathetic is that her sister-in-law believes Should-Doer enjoys playing the martyr. She doesn't even fully appreciate the things Should-Doer does. If Should-Doer said "no" more often, people would value her "yes" a lot more.

Secretive

Right-sided loops within ovals mean the writer deliberately hides information and feelings from others. (See Chapter 22 for all fourteen dishonesty indicators.)

If you're a Secretive, you have your reasons for not speaking your mind as much as you could. And you probably have a few touchy areas that make you nervous. You know what they are. Perhaps your job requires secrecy. Or you don't want to burden anyone with your pain. Perhaps you just like having a mysterious image.

Or maybe you lie. Maybe your lies are lily white and as simple as not telling your best friend you really hate her new haircut—even when she really wants your opinion. Maybe the lies are bigger.

But as a Secretive, you're not comfortable with those white or black lies. You'd rather escape the problems than deal with them, but know that's a losing proposition. Only by telling the complete truth will the burden grow lighter.

Anita Bryant, unloop those vowels!

Evasive

double loops

If left loops mean fibs to self, and right loops mean fibs to others, do loops on both sides might mean big trouble? Not necessarily. Locked up, loopy letters can reveal confusion about feelings. This could be a major stumbling block on the road to intimacy. Double looping is a sign that the writers are insecure and uncomfortable with themselves. If double loops combine with Thready writing (Chapter 14), watch out for manipulations!

If you're a double looper, you may be driving people away from you. Are you afraid that if you really expressed your anger, you'd tear a hole right out of the universe? Try telling your friends and family that you're angry when you're angry, instead of storing up all those frustrations until you feel as though you're going to explode.

You may imagine people don't like you even when they're crazy about you. If you suspect that may be true, check it out—instead of creating situations in which people do indeed leave you. Perhaps the crux of the matter is that you're not being quite honest within yourself about your feelings towards these other people.

Do you remember Hedy Lamarr? Surprised to find out she had this evasive trait in her handwriting?

Explosive

atmosphere, with
more about a

Inky ovals spell trouble. This writer tries to repress hostility—and fails. Handle this person as you would a smoking volcano. Watch out for hot lava. If this is your writing, try to resolve your angry feelings—punch pillows, run, or better still, go for some kind of counseling and find a way to work toward spiritual development. But do get hold of your temper before it takes you over!

If only the Soviets had known what Josef Stalin's explosive vowels meant.

ATTITUDES

Spacing reveals your attitudes about yourself, others and the world at large. And how you feel about yourself and others will influence your style. Here we'll be examining:
- letter width
- space between letters
- space between words and lines
- margin construction

Letter Width

Letter width reveals how you feel about yourself.

Scrunched letters

always trying too hard
and I can't be myself

Scrunched letter writers are too hard on themselves. The more you tightly scrunch your letters, the more harshly you judge yourself.

Wide letters

*am looking forward to rearing
om you if you feel that I*

Wide letters show a personality that is more accepting of itself. If this is your writing, you're willing to make a mistake now and then without crucifying yourself.

Spacing Between Letters

Spacing between letters within words reveals the writer's need for closeness or distance when relating one-on-one.

Crowded letters

*I have wondered if I w
parents . I was born in the*

Crowded letters reveal more caution than necesary. Is this you? You're introverted and don't like asking for the affection you really need. Maybe you don't know how to ask. You might just say, "How about a hug?"

CROWDED LETTERS AND THE SLANTERS

THINKER:	I know how to be close. I watch the Cosby Show.
JUGGLER:	Tell me what's on your mind so I can get back to work.
PLEASER:	Tell me what you're feeling so I can get back to work.
REACTOR:	My passion runs deeply within me, and there it stays.
MENDER:	"They're playing songs of love, but not for me . . ."
CHAMELEON:	If you tell me all your feelings, I'll tell you one of mine.

Widely spaced letters

a busy time
have the time

Widely spaced letters point out a free spirit who is outgoing and socially uninhibited. This is pure extroversion and vivacity, but it also reveals those who dissolve relationships as quickly as they create them. They're basically political creatures in the sense that they "know" which friendships to cultivate and which to leave alone.

WIDELY SPACED LETTERS AND THE SLANTERS

THINKER: It was nice seeing you, too, Fran . . . I mean Jan . . . I mean Ann.

JUGGLER: I'd marry you, but I don't think I can squeeze it into my schedule.

PLEASER: I'd marry you, but I have to take care of my mother.

REACTOR: Come here. Come here. Come here. Get back.

MENDER: Okay, let's go out. Are you free a month from next Wednesday?

CHAMELEON: I've planned a whole weekend—just you, me and the bowling team in Las Vegas!

Narrow letters, widely spaced

narrow letters wide

Narrow letters, widely spaced seem like a contradiction, but they're common. Writing this way means you've developed an uninhibited style, but when people make moves to get closer, you clam up.

NARROW LETTERS, WIDELY SPACED AND THE SLANTERS

THINKER: Yes, Terry and I have been engaged to be married for seven years now.

JUGGLER: When will I see you again? Let me check my appointment book. I think two weeks from Wednesday should be okay—I'll get back to you on that.

PLEASER: You didn't really expect—it's only our fifth date.

REACTOR: You didn't really expect—it's only our fiftieth date.

MENDER: I care about you, but I'm not sure I love you.

CHAMELEON: Let's get together after my return from Kenya, Greece and Nepal.

Wide letters, narrowly spaced

Wide letters narrowly spaced reveal writers who give themselves permission to make mistakes, but won't be that generous with you.

WIDE LETTERS NARROWLY SPACED AND THE SLANTERS

THINKER: If you weren't nagging me, I would have seen that car!

JUGGLER: If I weren't so busy running around town for you, I wouldn't have had to speed, and I wouldn't have hit that car.

PLEASER: All the crazies come out when I get behind the wheel. It's no wonder I rear-ended one of them.

REACTOR: People are always in my way. It was only a matter of time before someone would make me get into an accident.

MENDER: It's not my fault I hit that car, I was hurrying to meet you, and you know how upset you get when you have to wait.

CHAMELEON: The driver in front of me planned the whole thing. He slammed on his brakes, I couldn't avoid hitting him, and now he's going to sue me for whiplash.

Balanced space within and between letters

balanced spacing between

Balanced space within and between letters shows a flexible nature. If this is your writing, you relate to others honestly. And you probably take responsibility for your own problems.

BALANCED SPACE AND THE SLANTERS

With balanced spacing, the slant styles usually behave in their own most positive ways.

Spacing Between Words

Word spacing reflects the distance that we put between ourselves and society.

Narrow spaces between words

very narrow spaces between

These writers urgently want attention, and they're not picky in their ways of attracting it. They crave close contact, but they're often unwilling to reciprocate with their own time and energy when others need attention or favors from them. If this is your writing, look for the nonverbal clues people give that warn you when you're invading their privacy.

NARROW SPACING BETWEEN WORDS AND THE SLANTERS

THINKER: If you loved me, you wouldn't nag me all the time.

JUGGLER: If you loved me, you'd stop seeing Lee.

PLEASER: If you loved me, you'd stand up for me.

REACTOR: If you really and truly loved me, you'd slash that guy's tires.

MENDER: If you loved me, you'd want to listen to my problems.

CHAMELEON: If you loved me, you wouldn't ask me to quit the roller derby team.

Wide letters and spaces within the same word

Marcia told

These writers keep wide distances between themselves and others. If this is your writing, you're either moody and depressed, or you don't feel that you're important in anyone's life.

You may yearn for and try to get constant attention, feeling that if you aren't seen, heard and acknowledged, you'll be forgotten and abandoned. But you don't know what to do with all that attention when you get it. The more you become involved with others and their needs, turning your sensitivity away from yourself and the more you reach out, the more people will value your company.

Andy Warhol signed his name with wide letters and wide spaces.

WIDE LETTERS AND WIDE SPACES BETWEEN WORDS AND THE SLANTERS

Let's say a Scout Reunion is announced in the local papers. Anyone who was ever a Brownie, Cub, Girl or Boy Scout is invited. Here are each slanters' responses:

THINKER: Who cares?

JUGGLER: I'm too busy . . . but everyone will miss me if I don't go. Okay. I'll go.

PLEASER: I'd love to go, but I'm too fat to fit in the old uniform.

REACTOR: Oh boy! I can't wait!

MENDER: If I can't find my old badges, I'm not going.

CHAMELEON: What's a "Scout?"

Narrow letters with minimal space between words

Narrow letters with minimal spacing

This spacing reveals fear and dependence. These are writers whose feelings are tangled into those of other people just as their letters and words are. When dealing with them, it's important to be direct, because they're oblivious to nonverbal signals— such as people turn-ing their backs or not returning their handshake. You can't be sub-tle with them.

If you tightly space letters and words, you may be ignoring other people's needs without realizing it—or maybe you just don't care whether or not you're imposing on your friends. If you don't open your eyes, you may find you don't have many friends left.

NARROW LETTERS WITH TINY SPACES BETWEEN WORDS AND THE SLANTERS

THINKER: I'll agree to separate vacations, but only if we go to the same city.

JUGGLER: I know it's our wedding night, but I'm not about to skip my acting class.

PLEASER: Why do you always lock the bathroom door?

REACTOR: I miss you when you're sleeping. You do dream about me, don't you?

MENDER: I know you told me yesterday you wouldn't be home for dinner tonight, but I fixed your favorite dinner anyway.

Chameleons couldn't write with close word and letter spacing if their lives depended on it.

Wide letters with wide spaces between words

wide letters and

You know the guy at the ball park who reaches over the fence and snatches the ball in play? He writes like this. His team may lose a home run because of what he did, but so what? He doesn't care. He's getting what he wants.

In general, these writers insist on getting their way. If they aren't being noticed, they feel something is drastically wrong—with *you* for not paying attention.

WIDE LETTERS WITH WIDE SPACES
BETWEEN WORDS AND THE SLANTERS

THINKER: What do you mean? A pair of aces beats a full house—
doesn't it?

JUGGLER: It's only midnight. Aren't you going to stay and look
at my vacation pictures?

PLEASER: You didn't want me to sing at your party last night?

REACTOR: To heck with the budget! I've got to have that new
Porsche!

MENDER: If I can't get my way, I won't pay!

CHAMELEON: But I thought the folks at the retirement home would
like to arm wrestle!

Well balanced spacing

Here is the social grace of Loretta Young together with the sensitivity
of Dr. Spock. If this is your writing, you have social maturity, intelligence, flexibility and an organized way of thinking. Hooray for
you. If you want to look for areas to improve in your life, maybe
you have a few "Red Lights." See Chapter 21.

Controlled spacing

If every word is spaced exactly the same, the writers fear the unexpected and would like to lead predictable and very controlled lives.
Don't you get the impression that their true feelings are also kept
under strict control? The images we behold are surely not a reflection of their true, inner natures.

Drastically uneven spacing

It has an odd writing a full-page to some

These writers are the exact opposite of the controlled spacers. Instead of maintaining the appearance of serenity, their moods override everything arround them. You'll think you're their best friend one moment, and the next you'll wonder what you said to receive such a cold shoulder.

If this is your writing, try monitoring your behavior to see whether you can achieve more consistency in your responses and reactions to others.

Spacing Between the Lines

Look at line spacing to judge how involved people want to be with those around them.

Crowded lines and/or tangled lines

types positions. I recently finished accounting courses in order to be elegible for a more

Crowded and/or tangled lines betray confused thoughts and feelings. This may be only a temporary condition, but if the writing is chronically tangled, the writer needs some kind of support or counseling.

Often when these writers are willing to take full responsibility for some of their problems, solutions are easy to come by. For example, when clients who tangle lines complain of loneliness, I ask them what they're doing about it. They often admit that they're hermits. Then they laugh at the contradiction between desire and behavior and promise that they'll join this or that group. One client reported back six months later saying she found a lot of new friends with the Anti-Vivisectionists.

Large distances between lines

Many businesses that can be

run from the home start

Here we find very little interaction between the writers and their surroundings. They have isolated themselves with fantasies that could keep Steven Spielberg filming for years. Their schemes are far-fetched, sometimes perhaps even a bit paranoid. And because they shy away from close contact with others, they're likely to stray farther and farther from reality. A caring family member or friend may need to get involved and help this person find more interests and responsibilities in the Now.

Balanced spacing

I just moved in from New York City in July and presently unemployed. I

Balanced spaces between lines reflect clear thinking. These writers socialize when, where and with whom they please. They don't join in out of loneliness, and their friends generally value their company.

Margin Construction

Think of a page of writing as representing the world. The margins you establish set up your place in that world and show how you feel about it. The left margin represents the past. The distance you place between the left edge of the page and where you begin each line shows how you feel about your past. And the opposite holds true. Where you end each line at the right side of the paper reveals how you feel about your future. Top and bottom margins reflect your relationship to society. Are you stiff and formal, relying on appearances and conventional behavior? Or are you careless and casual about others?

Balanced Margins

These writers respect their own and others' territories. In addition, they care deeply about the way things look. They like new shoes, clean rooms, a decorated work space, and they'd never think of walking to the corner in their pajamas to fetch the daily paper— unless they're Chameleons.

Wide Left Margin

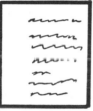

People who are confident about the future, who see their place within it and don't look back at their mistakes, write with a wide left margin. Not only won't they look back, they don't even want to be reminded of the past. *Note:* Can you imagine this writer in a close relationship with a Mender, who lives in the past?

Wide Right Margin

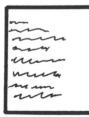

Reserved, frightened and self-conscious people create wide right margins. These writers stay with tyrant bosses because they don't think they'll be able to find other jobs. They keep dating people who don't want marriage (though they would like to get married) out of fear of loneliness. This set-up almost always indicates the rejection of motherly, nurturing love. That's why the writers associate with difficult, aloof people. They would like to have a workable or loving relationship, but they don't know how to achieve it.

Island Margins

If a wide right margin means fear of the future and a wide left margin means escape from the past, having wide margins all around means these writers can't go forward and can't go backward. They're stuck in the middle and have nowhere to go. It's as though they're waiting for something to happen instead of making things happen for themselves. They need to motivate themselves to become more sociable so they won't be permanently isolated.

Creeping Left Margin

A left margin that grows wider as the page continues reveals a personality that loves to plan ahead. And once those plans are made, heaven help the person who gets in the way. Full speed ahead!

Retreating Left Margin

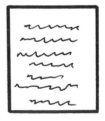

No matter how these writers try to release past failures and disappointments, they have a hard time letting go. They hang onto everything that ever went wrong in their lives, and by doing that, they paralyze their own future.

Ragged Left Margin

You've read about the Chameleon in Chapter I: Everything that applies to Chameleons applies to these margins. These writers disregard all commonly held social values just to be known as eccentric people. They're unpredictable and lack solid values. This is the true rebel without a cause.

**Ragged
Right Margin**

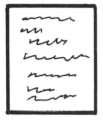

There's a big difference between this writer and the one before. The ragged left margin makers are overtly defiant and rebellious. the ragged right margin makers are simply *impulsively* unpredictable. They get so excited about tomorrow's plans that they forget they promised to be somewhere else.

Once they acknowledge the fact that their plans are likely to change at the last minute, they can make life much easier by setting up only tentative plans with their friends. This will make them feel less guilty for not following through and provide others with realistic expectations.

**Solid Writing:
No Margins**

These writers' enemies are Silence, Solitude and Death. In order to evade these villains, they occupy themselves with hundreds of insignificant details, wasting their time and everyone else's. They plan too much, talk too much and stick their noses into everyone's business. People either hate these writers or love them.

Large Upper Margin

If, in a letter, "Dear _____" begins more than three inches from the top of the page, that friend has a great deal of respect for you and people in general.

No Upper Margin

If you get that letter from a friend and "Dear _____" begins right at the upper edge, be careful. This writer is revealing a lack of respect for you and your feelings. Beware of Trojan horses!

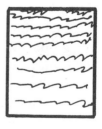

Large Lower Margin

These writers are isolated and out of touch with society. Avoiding contact with the world at large, they see themselves as vaguely odd and at present, at least, are not trying to fit in.

No Lower Margin

A very narrow bottom margin reveals an individual who wants to have people around most of the time. This could be a warning of depression, so look for drooping letters and lines.

COMMUNICATION CLUSTERS

You may have noticed that each section of this chapter describes the same communication styles again and again. For instance, if you have open vowels, you probably also have very tight spacing between words. Both indicate your urgent need to express yourself.

Many writing styles are often found together in the same handwriting. Here are a few of the most common combinations:

• Open vowels
• Medium width letters
• Balanced spacing between letters, words, lines and margins
Meaning: Poised and socially comfortable, aware of how to give and take gracefully.

• Wide open vowels
• Medium to wide letters
• Narrowly spaced words
• Tangled lines

- Advancing left margin
- Small lower margin

Meaning: Lacks awareness of social boundaries.

- Closed ovals
- Narrow letters
- Narrowly spaced letters
- Widely spaced words
- Wide left and upper margins

Meaning: Hesitation about getting close and making meaningful commitments.

- Left-looped ovals
- Controlled and even spacing
- Perfectly spaced and untangled lines
- Perfect, even margins

Meaning: These writers are unsure of who they are and how they fit into their environment. Their behavior is likely to be predictable, because they don't usually take chances. Often this approach to life is boring, so these writers are likely to wear out their welcome as they try to get close.

- Right-looped ovals
- Widely spaced letters
- Closely spaced words and lines
- Narrowing left margin or no margins

Meaning: Lonely people who want to be close but alienate others in the process. They aren't direct in stating what they need, and often get angry because those around them aren't mindreaders.

- Explosive vowels
- Irregular letter, word and line spacing
- Wide letters
- Narrowly spaced words
- Ragged left margin

Meaning: Disturbed personality. Handle with care.

19. Love and Sexuality: Lower Zone and Pressure

Are you sure you don't want to start reading this book on the first page? I know—silly question!

When we talk about the many expressions of love and sexuality, a number of factors must be taken into consideration. We're going to look at the lower zone—all the strokes that occur below the baseline—and at pen pressure. So don't look below the line, notice full, voluptuous lower loops and assume that person who just handed you that note belongs in an X-rated movie. You also need to consider spacing, basic handwriting shape and slant before you can begin to evaluate what's going on.

Many people ask whether homosexuality can be spotted in handwriting. Not easily. All you can tell for sure from handwriting analysis is whether the individuals are comfortable with their choices. As you study the following lower loop styles, be aware that the more angular or retraced the loop, the more uncomfortable the writer is with sexual matters.

THE LOWER LOOPS

The place to begin is below the baseline, looking at the size, shape and presence of all the lower loops: "j's", "g's", "y's" and "z's." Why look at loops? Because they stand for imagination. Loops below the line represent sexual, social and financial imagination. Large loops that sweep back and finish above the word tell you the writer is highly social and highly sexed. Narrow loops makers are more inhibited than full-loop makers. Non-loops don't mean the writers aren't interested in love or sex. It just means they're practical about it. It also means they won't spend a great deal of time thinking about or planning for romantic evenings. They put other things first—most of the time.

 Large loops that finish high   **Narrow loops**   **Non-loops**

Classic Loops

If your lower loops are double the length of the middle zone height and finish *at* the baseline, your sexual appetite is average. A stroke rising higher than the baseline (as the "y" does) expresses optimism, like President Reagan's.

Full Loops

Full, long lower loops reveal pizzazz. You need variety—sexually and socially. You tend to get bored, so you may want to put a little extra into keeping things interesting, the way Harry Houdini did.

Dominant Loops

Here is a preoccupation with romance and sex that you can spot miles away. These lower loops are so large, the rest of the writing looks small in comparison. In fact, to qualify as a Dominant Looper, the loops must be at least 4 times longer than the middle zone is high.

If these are your loops, you're a very restless person. You seek variety in your love and social life, and you don't know quite what to do with all your extra energy.

With these exaggerated lower loops you tend to store emotions instead of expressing them. It's like having a lot of love that you need to pass along, but with no one there to receive it. Even if someone is there to give it to, you still store more than you give. Maybe that's why dominant looper Jerry Lewis seems to have so much to give to his audiences.

No Loops or Shriveled Loops

Shriveled loops or loopless dangles indicate that these writers channel their energy into work, religion, spirituality or daily routines. Interest in love, sex and social life lag behind other concerns. If this is your writing, be aware that you're turning away from a major part of life—not only love, but other drives as well.

Jesse Jackson writes with shriveled loops. Perhaps that's one reason why his private life is so extremely private.

Left Roving Loops

Leftward roving loops reveal that the writer feels guilty when it comes to expressing love physically. These people may also feel they don't deserve having close friends or a nice savings account. (They're the ones to approach on your next charity drive, but you'll have to find Pat Nixon and Anita Bryant yourself.)

Right Roving Loops

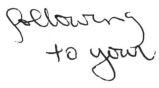

Rightward roving loops show that the writer is overly concerned about the future—particularly the outlook for love and money. It's usually a temporary handwriting trait, so don't worry about worrying if you make your lower loops this way. Tell John Lindsay not to worry either.

Long, Thin Loops

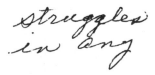

Pony tail loops, long and narrow, say you're ultra-careful when choosing a friend or mate. You're perfectly justified in having that attitude these days, but you do find it difficult to accept people in general. You may have one small set of friends and shy away from expanding your sphere.

Sigmund Freud made his skinny lower loops so long that they tangled into the lines below.

Tiny Bottom Loops

With tiny lower loops, you're sure to mistrust the motives of others and take a *very* long time to feel at ease. You'd do best to work alone or work for yourself.

Drooping Loops

The droopy looper is a discouraged person who feels like a failure and is pessimistic about future finances. If these are your loops, don't worry. It's usually a temporary condition. George Washington sometimes had droopy loops, too.

Upreaching and Leftward Loops

A loop that sweeps past the baseline and ends pointing toward the left means the writer needs attention, approval and recognition in social and romantic situations.

No Lower Loops

If you don't make lower loops at all, you're blocking out a great part of the enjoyment of life. You say you'd rather read a good book than go to a party. In fact, you're spending most of your time alone. Are you surprised that Burt Reynolds doesn't make lower loops? I was. Elvis Presley didn't make lower loops either.

Barbed Endings

Finding barbs at the bottoms of lower non-loops is a warning that you're blaming other people for the fustrations you feel. If you do have a problem that involves your relationships with others, it's important to realize that only you can change the situation—all appearances to the contrary!

Mass murderer, David Berkowitz, Son of Sam, put barbs on all his lower endings.

Retraced Loops

Fully retraced loops say the writer is inhibited socially and sexually. If these are your loops, you feel under pressure to guard your feelings. You're repressing the need to express yourself on many levels.

Crossed & Disconnected Loops

Making a cross at the baseline with a disconnected lower loop is a definite signal that you feel inadequate in social situations and in love relationships. It's a sign of sadness in general.

This trait if often found in the handwriting of the spouses of alcoholics. They may be taking the blame for their partners' dysfunction.

Robert and Edward Kennedy both made their final "y's" this way.

Twisted Angular Loops

These triangulated loops show a person who resents being told what to do. You may have your own unique ideas about what is proper and what isn't and blame others when they don't perform as you think they should. You may be edgy and defensive in many areas of your life. To overcome these obstacles, you need to lighten up on your expectations from others, realizing that other people don't think and act as you do, and it's all right if they don't. But it may help to be aware that others tend to see you as a hostile person, and perhaps go a little out of your way to show your good will.

Joe McCarthy, Jack Dempsey, Hubert H. Humphrey and Martin Luther King, Jr. all twisted the lower loops in their signatures.

Atilla Non-Loops

This angular non-loop juts off at a rightward angle and should be considered carefully. If the rest of the writing is sharp, jagged and tight, the writer could be violent. But if the rest of the writing is garland (Chapter 14), it simply means these writers are actively and self-reliantly pursuing goals. Dr. George Bach, author of *Creative Aggression*, signs his name this way.

PRESSURE

To determine energy levels, or vitality, you need to look at the amount of pressure the writer used to apply ink to the page. Simply feel the back of the page if a ball point pen or pencil was used. If you can feel the writing like an embossment, there's a tremendous amount of energy. This is the Sensualist. If you don't feel the writing on the back of the page, and the writing itself looks wispy and leaves trails of ink, the writers lack vitality. We'll refer to them as Fragile. If the writing falls somewhere between these two depths, the individuals will be closer to average in energy. We'll call them "Able." If the pressure varies, all levels of energy will be present, and we'll call them "Moody." And there's more.

Fragile

As you may have guessed, a Fragile doesn't have either the strength or the desire for an intense relationship. If this is your writing you're a soft-hearted, sensitive person who avoids conflict. If eating ice cream can be related to romance, you're content with one scoop.

Able

*spurs that jingle jangle jingle
Know the rest of this song*

Ables usually have moderate energy, moderate drives and moderate appetites. They may buy gym memberships, go a few times, spend most of their visit in the hot tub, and then let their memberships expire. It's not that they don't like to exercise—it's just that they seldom get intense about anything.

Sensualist

*hard to comprehend. Can
someone else's actions are
we that right.*

Sensualists give all their energy to everything they do. If they run, they run ten miles a day. If they play games, they play to win. If they're out to win someone's heart, they won't stop working at it and flirting until they're married—and sometimes they'll continue for the next 50 years or more!

If you're a Sensualist, you're a devoted slave to the things in your life that mean the most to you. If you get into fashion, for example, you'll wear the latest designer clothes. If you get into entertaining, your parties will be talked about for weeks afterwards. You may be into eating in a heavy way, have a subscription to *Food and Wine*, and dine in the best-reviewed restaurants. In music, your tastes generally tend toward exotic, ethnic or hard rock sounds.

Moody

fluctuating

If your writing fluctuates in pressure, it indicates erratic moods. This writing is sometimes associated with hypoglycemia. It's not possible to predict your energy level except to say it changes at the drop of a hat.

DANGER SIGNALS

Smudgy

This writer may be prone to violence. Some heavily smudged writing has been linked to criminal acts, but this of course depends upon the rest of the writing. In some cases, it indicates unpredictability. In others it means you have artistic talent, or a leaky ballpoint pen. Maybe you're Sirhan Sirhan.

Blunt

Blunt endings on the last letters of many words may also be an indication of violent behavior. Think of it as a caveman's club, and examine the rest of the writing carefully. Henry Fonda's handwriting was full of clubs, and those who worked closely with him say he was very difficult to get along with. They say he was a walking hornet's nest, because he was always losing his temper over trivial things.

20. Green Lights

Green lights are handwriting traits that give you the good news. They reveal positive traits and abilities, such as confidence levels, sense of humor, imagination and optimism. We'll talk about open-mindedness, generosity and will power. We'll also look at family ties because in many cases your feelings about your original family effect how you feel about creating a new family. We'll look at some other traits, too. Have you been flipping through the pages looking for i-dots and t-bars? (Most people do.) They're here.

CONFIDENCE: Capitals

Through research, some psychologists have become convinced that the first thing we respond to when we meet others is whether they are more, less or equal to us in self-confidence. Why? Most of us want to know if we measure up. We ask ourselves: Am I *as* pretty? Am I *as* smart? Am I *as* popular? Am I *as* accomplished?

People are like chickens in that we establish a pecking order. And we don't want to admit that we feel last in line for the rooster. We're self-conscious, and sometimes fearful, animals. When we meet other people, we're hoping we won't be judged unworthy of their company. So we examine how they judge themselves. And when we find a person who lacks confidence (we recognize it almost at once), we immediately feel better about ourselves. We think we'll get the added bonus that the other person will look up to us! Of course, it doesn't always work that way, especially when an unconfident person tries to make a truly confident one look bad.

To determine confidence in handwriting, look at the height of the upper-case letter in relation to lower case letters. The most important capital letter is the personal pronoun "I." Next examine the capital letters in the writer's signature. Signatures are tricky, though, because they show how people *want* to appear—not necessarily the way they actually are. So look at the capital "I" first.

Also notice the size of the initial capitals when people write *your* name. If those initial letters equal the size of their own initials, they consider you their equal. If they make your initial capitals smaller than theirs, you don't rate very high. The opposite is true: if your initials appear larger than theirs, they're looking up to you.

Proportionate Capitals

This sample shows confidence. The capital "I" and other upper case letters are twice as tall as the lower case letters. If this is your writing, you have grace, charm and self-confidence. You don't need the approval of others for everything you do. When you go to a party, you neither sit alone in a corner hoping to be noticed, nor do you feel the need to dance on the buffet table, and you aren't afraid to introduce yourself when you see someone you want to meet.

Short Capitals

These upper case letters are nearly the same height as the lower case letters. If you make these insignificant capitals, your low self-esteem is showing. When you think about attempting a task, you may not feel up to it unless someone comes along and says, "Hey, of course you can do it. Go for it!" and gives you a push. Most of the time, you're your own worst enemy. When in doubt—try—take a chance! You'll never know unless you do.

Oversized Capitals

This is a longer Im

This is another example of writing that reveals low self-esteem. Surprised? If you write oversized capitals, it means you're bluffing about your self-confidence. You're unsure of yourself, but you make yourself stand tall and speak in a strong, clear voice anyway. If the lower case "i's" throughout your handwriting are diminished in size, or you carelessly omit a few of them, you're already aware that you don't feel as good about yourself as you pretend.

You have a "fake it till you make it" approach to self-esteem that sometimes fails you. For instance, if you were to go to a party where you didn't know most of the guests, you wouldn't be shy about telling a joke or story to the group. But it would be more difficult for you to approach a person you were attracted to without being introduced. And if you wanted to see that someone again, you'd be inclined to let it go, unless you received a great deal of encouragement.

IMAGINATION: Loops

Loops and i-dots show imagination: Upper loops reveal intellectual imagination and emotion while i-dots represent other related qualities.

The L's

Skinny	Medium	Fat
please	*Please*	*help*

These "l's" reflect the uses of imagination, from the limited skinny-looped type to the moderate-sized kind to the dramatic fat "l." The loopier the "l," the freer the imagination.

The D's

Loops don't belong in the "d." However, a good 80% of the population writes with them. The looped "d" reveals a sensitivity to criticism. If you loop your "d's," you often imagine criticism where none is intended, and may even take someone else's side in arguments against yourself! You'll go so far as to contradict yourself in order to appear right. This aversion to criticism forces you to do things so well that no one will have an opportunity to put you down. How can anyone condemn perfection?

The T's

Loops don't belong in the "t" either. Here again, people who write with t-loops are using their imaginations against themselves. T-loopers are sensitive about their *work* performance, while they seem able to handle personal criticism quite well (unless "d's" are looped.)

The H's

Lower case h-loopers may hold onto rigid religious beliefs without questioning their current validity. It's a sign of blind faith. If this is your h-loop, do you ever question your beliefs?

IMAGINATION: The i-Dots

High Dots

You're high-flying—idealistic, enthusiastic and imaginative.

Advanced Dots

You relentlessly pursue your goals and have a tad more curiosity and enthusiasm than even the high dot writer.

Perfect Dots

You're a perfectionist—a stickler for details— capable of enduring loyalty.

No Dots

You're absentminded and more than likely forget your own phone number.

Circled Dots

Circled dots indicate a couple of things: First, you want attention, but don't want to put forth a great deal of effort to get it. Second, you enjoy experimenting with the way you look and toying with new ideas.

Open Left Dots

Dots that open and face left indicate neurosis.

Open Right Dots

You're highly observant and perceptive. Sherlock Holmes would have made open right-facing dots.

Dashing Dots

You're likely to be sarcastic. "Gee, that smells delicious—who came over to cook it?" This is a dot Don Rickles would be proud of.

Left Dots

Here's the procrastinator's dot. If you also cross your "t's" to the left, it's your inclination to put things off until the last possible moment. Going to the theater with you means missing every opening scene.

Forward Dots

You anticipate needs before they exist. Your mind is always way ahead of the game.

OPTIMISM: t-Bars and Line Slant

Optimism and pessimism are revealed through t-bar length and slant.

Balanced Bar

This bar is perfectly balanced on the stem with constant pressure from start to finish. If this is your t-bar, you're an excellent planner.

Upward Bar

You frantically drive yourself towards success. And you think everyone should be as excited about your goals as you are.

Downward Bar

You tend to dominate other people, and you may walk over others if you aren't careful.

Small Even Bar

You're conservative and careful.

Plane-Wing Bar

This airplane-wingish t-bar shows irrepressible optimism.

Low Bars

You need to raise your goals. This may also be a temporary condition revealing that you feel defeated because of a work-related disappointment.

I've heard about one fellow who crossed t's *below* the line. He was a gravedigger. Honest.

Long & High Bar   You have a splendid imagination, and you're an idealist.

Right Half Bar   You're busy planning tomorrow today.

Left Half Bar   "I'll get to it tomorrow, or the next day"—famous last words.

Curvy Bar   You think life is just for having fun.

Fish Hook Bar   You love to collect things. If the hook is on the right, you may be greedy for attention and anxious for praise. If the hook is on the left, it means you see yourself striking it rich in the near future.

Convex (Arch) Bar   You're actively trying to control your faults. Good luck.

Concave (Bowl) Bar   You find more comfort in following than leading. You go along with other people's goals, and don't take your own seriously. Why are you so ready to jump on other people's bandwagons? Usually you don't give yourself credit for having the talent and ability to carry through your own projects.

Star Bar

You hate to waste money and ink. And you try to take the shortest path to your goals because you don't like to waste time either.

Looped Star Bar

You're every bit as responsible as the Star Bar above, but more strong-willed. This loop reveals persistence.

Sharp Bar

You hate to waste money and ink. And you

Any sharp-ending t-bar reveals the need to dominate others in order to get your way.

Left Ending Bar

Ending t-bars to the left means you're pre-occupied with yourself. You may get jealous easily or succumb to self-pity.

Uncrossed Bar

The uncrossed "t" at the end of a word means you're hypersensitive, and not only to feelings. You're also able to detect odors no one else notices.

ENTHUSIASM: The Lines

You can determine enthusiasm from the slant of the baseline. On unlined paper, writing should travel straight across the page, but it might have many variations:

Straight Lines

This example reveals controlled and moderate enthusiasm. It goes neither up nor down. If this is your writing level, you have an even temper and are quite reliable. You may be a stabilizing influence on people or bore them, depending upon your relationship and other writing factors.

Upsloping Lines

people today want to allow other to do their own thing and don't want to judge them, even if it is obviously evil.

Writing that climbs up the page demonstrates enthusiasm. If this is your line slant, you may have unrealistic expectations for yourself, others and situations in which you believe you can get ahead without making an effort. It also means you're easily disappointed. If your writing climbs the page wildly, watch for drastic mood swings. That optimism isn't grounded, and many people don't believe that you can be as naive as you appear.

Down Sloping Lines

I don't have any time for anymore

Handwriting sliding down the page shows depression—either temporary or chronic. It may also indicate fatigue.

Petering Out Lines

I don't have any employees on boa

If your writing begins going up and then comes back down, it means your enthusiasm starts high in the beginning, but is often lost in the middle of a project.

Picking Up Lines

Hi! My name is Dominique. I'm 13 years old and my birthday is on

If your writing goes down and then starts up, it means you start things with a pessimistic attitude. Then, somewhere in the middle of the project when you see things aren't going so badly, you get a second wind and pick up tempo.

SENSE OF HUMOR

Some of the best fun we have is finding humor in unlikely places—and simply laughing. And unless we laugh in the wrong places at a movie, or during a lecture, no one will mind how much we indulge ourselves. A sense of humor line looks like a smile. You can find it in the crossing of a "t," the dotting of an "i," the underscoring of a name, the stroke introducing a capital "M" or "N," and connections between letters.

The opposite holds true. Critical and rigid people stab the baseline with jabs.

Know, too, that people who connect letters and words with soft strokes are more than likely to be kind.

OPEN AND CLOSED-MINDEDNESS: The e's

Open and Closed E's

Open "e's" indicate open-mindedness; closed "e's," closed-mindedness. "E's" are like eyeballs. Are they open or shut?

Open "e" people are open to suggestions and see possibilities everywhere—maybe in too many places.

Closed "e" people have rigid ideas and don't often see that there are possibilities right in front of their faces. However, closed "e's" also indicate a powerful ability to concentrate.

COURAGE: The s's

Rounded "S"

A rounded lower case "s" means you're apt to toss your values aside if they come into conflict with your popularity. The more pointed your "s" and "p," the less likely you are to be manipulated away from your own track.

GENEROSITY: Word Endings

Generosity shows up in the length of word-endings. The longer the tail at the end of the word, the greater your generosity. If there aren't any word tails, you're more practical where generosity is concerned. Also look at spacing. The tighter you pack your letters together, the closer you are to Ebenezer Scrooge. Looser letter spacing is more generous.

FAMILY TIES: Lead-Ins

Look for a short introductory stroke that leads into the body of a word. It's truly a good indication to find. It means that family is important to these writers, but they won't make an issue of it. If this is your writing, you're mature, practical and take the shortest route to accomplishing your goals. Some people think you have four hands because you seem to get more done in one hour than three people can in a whole afternoon. You have initiative plus.

Wavy Lead-In

Family is very important to these writers, too. They will do all they can to help their families when necessary. If this is your writing, you're a responsive, loving and communicative person. But you need a good push to get you started on new projects.

Long Wavy Lead-In

Again, family is very important here. This introductory stroke is also the sense of humor stroke. If this is your stroke, you're probably light on your feet on the dance floor, but not so swift at getting started elsewhere. You're apt to manicure your toenails, weed and fertilize the grass and wrestle with the dog before getting to work.

Saggy Lead-In

Family is a source of guilt for these writers. They usually feel they could be doing much more for their mothers, sisters, brothers, cousins, aunts, uncles, grandparents, in-laws, etc., and should be.

If this is your writing, you need to develop shortcuts in all areas of your life. You're aware that some people can talk on the phone, pay the bills, brew coffee and ride an exercise bike at the same time? Well, as this writer, you can't, won't and don't want to.

Umbrella Lead-In

These writers won't reveal family secrets. They feel there's something to hide and may be uncomfortable about an alcoholic brother, a schizophrenic mother or a blue collar father. If this is your writing, you're stuck in a rut and find it difficult to adapt to new situations. Don't try so hard to be perfect.

Angular Lead-In

The past is never far from these writers' minds, and it's not a source of pleasure. They feel a great deal of anger and hostility for one or more family members. Perhaps they feel someone cheated them out of their rightful inheritance. If this is your writing, you need to let go of the past in order to get into today.

Thready Lead-In

The past hounds these writers, too, but they're not sure how they feel about it. Their family confuses them: Where do they fit in? Maybe mother *says* she loves you best, but consistently rewards a brother or sister.

Very Long Thready Lead-In

These writers are vague about their families and don't clearly present all the facts. If you hear, "My brother is on a long vacation," inquire about how the food really is in Folsom Prison.

On the job, these writers seldom buckle down to work. They think it's their job to make sure their co-workers are having fun, but they're actually wasting everyone's time in the process.

Hook Lead-In

There's a strong love of family here, but these writers are far too attached to their original families. In a man's writing it's difficult for him to feel that his own wife and children are his *real* family. In a woman's writing, she may feel that her mother is her own child's *real* mother.

If this is your writing, you continually relate to your past experiences in order to solve present problems.

Barbed Lead-In

This piece of barbed wire stuck on the beginning of a word is usually temporary. It's similar to the sense of humor "smile" because it's a lead-in, but it's straight, not curved. This little lead-in indicates temper, irritation and, possibly, arrogance.

Lead-In
From Below

These writers resent their families for holding them back or causing them grief. This resentment can cripple goals and weaken family ties.

INITIATIVE: Lead-Ins

Lead-in From Above on Upper Case Letters

These writers are smart and know it. They also want everyone else to know it.

Umbrella Lead-In
on Upper
Case Letters

If this is the lead-in into your name or to many of your upper case letters, you've got a wonderful imagination. However, it also reveals that you may be covering up your insecurities, because you don't want other people to think that you sometimes feel unsure of yourself.

Angular Lead-In on Upper And Lower Case Letters

This writer has an amazing capacity for coming up with new ideas.

21. Red Lights

Red lights are handwriting signals that whisper or shout, "I have a problem." Most handwriting contains some or many red lights because we all think we need the defenses red lights give us. They are the buffers we create to protect our vulnerable points.

Red Light traits fall into two categories: psychological defenses and downright aggression. Some are tolerable; others are obnoxious. Guilt is a popular red light, and in some cases it's deadly. Instability, insecurity, self-consciousness, overdependence are all red lights. So are depression, pride, resentment, miserliness, and the tendency to see yourself as a victim. All of them—especially temper, jealousy, hostility, violence, pathological lying and sadism—can be serious indeed.

Guilt

Mender slant   **Leftward downstrokes**   **Left lower loops**

Leftward upper zone strokes

All these handwriting characteristics demonstrate guilt. Any stroke that glides, sweeps, swings, or plunges towards the left in any zone says the writer has guilt feelings. Almost all writing has some degree of guilt, because it's almost impossible to write without travelling somewhat to the left, and it's almost impossible not to succumb to feeling guilty sometimes.

Menders' writing always slants left and they are usually fraught with guilt. Thinkers and right-slanters often make leftward downstrokes in m, n, and h formations. Since these letters occupy the middle zone, it means the writers have guilt in their social life.

Left-swaying lower loops indicate guilt over money or intimacy. Left lower-loopers may not feel they deserve to express physical love. Or they feel guilty for making or spending money.

Left upper-zone strokes indicate spiritual, religious or philosophical guilt. These writers generally feel secure with the values they learned within their families and are apt to feel guilty for something like sleeping in on the Sabbath, for example, instead of going to church or temple.

Guilt is a paradox because it makes generous people self-obsessed. What? How can that be? Because guilt-feeling people are generous in a self-righteous way. When things go wrong, they grab all the blame for themselves. You've heard, "It's *all* my fault," haven't you? And believing everything is under *their* control means they assume they possess superhuman power.

Pleasers and Reactors often enjoy inflicting guilt on others. Thinkers try to help people discover ways to overcome guilt, and Jugglers are too busy to be bothered with someone else's guilt. Forget Chameleons—most of them don't know the meaning of guilt. Don't overlook spacing between letters and words. The balanced spacer of any slant is patient when others feel guilty.

Passive Aggression

Let's say your mother-in-law hates you because you say what's on your mind. But she never confronts you directly because she doesn't want to alienate her child. Her secret weapon is that she's aware of your Achilles' heel: You detest performing on the piano at parties. How does she get at you and make herself look great in the process? She throws a party, invites you, and when everyone is having a merry time, annouces that you play the piano and give great sing-alongs. Then, when you refuse to play in front of all her guests, guess what? You're the petulant child and she's the Victimized Mother-in-law. You lose—she wins.

Some people develop passive aggression into a fine art whereby they get even by making others feel two inches tall. Why would anyone do that? Because passive aggressive people don't want to admit they have hostile feelings. And so they disguise aggressive acts so that they appear benevolent. It's a set-up.

Look for fake garlands or retraced scallops resting on the baseline, and you've found a passive aggressive writer. Study the sample carefully because you'll find this writing style often.

Instability

consulting.

I love the industry and look forward to an opportunity

Nobody's perfect, but we can sometimes wear overselves out trying to deal with the emotional instability of others. If you can't count on the emotional health of your friend or child, you'll never want to get out of bed and deal with them. Instability makes itself known in lack of willpower, sloppiness and hyper-emotionality. This is reflected in an unsteady baseline.

Note: An unsteady baseline may also indicate a nutritional disorder, and it's difficult to tell the difference. It's a chicken-and-egg enigma. Is the person unbalanced because of a nutritional deficiency or is it the other way around?

If your own baseline is unwaveringly straight and your spacing is tight, you may not be able to cope the instability of your friend, child or work partner. Try getting the unstable individual to take the test for hypoglycemia. Then if nutrition is involved, a proper food plan can be worked out and the moods may level out.

Insecurity

more often than

Insecurity may make it impossible for you to feel close—whether it's you or your friend who is insecure. This trait is known as the "Shark's Tooth," because it imparts a biting edge to the personality.

It's easy to spot in handwriting. Look for caved-in "h's" and "n's" and "m's." If your mate, boss or friend has this trait, that snapping at you comes from their insecurity—not anything you did or said. Now you know.

Self-Consciousness   *m*   or   *M*

When the last "m" or "n" hump rises higher than the initial humps, the writers will be self-conscious and uncomfortable about their bodies. If they act or do public speaking, they'll sometimes feel that the audience can see through their clothes. They almost always complain about their weight.

If this is your writing, you believe you should be exactly as everyone else wants you to be. You value the opinions of others over your own, and seldom will you dare to be original or spontaneous. It's easier to keep your deepest feelings neatly tucked away where no one can get to them.

I know two women who make these self-conscious "m's." Both drastically underrate themselves and both have a capital M in their names. Maria is gradually getting over her self-consciousness through starting her own home-based manufacturing business. It wasn't until she started speaking in public about her product, an educational toy, and getting large orders, that she began to realize her value. As she overcame her fears (she now calls on major amusement parks, zoos and the media to promote her unusual product), her M-humps began to level out.

Ms. M., the other woman, is an artist in a cooperative studio.

Without the protection she feels from the group, it's unlikely she'd continue painting. She has not overcome her self-consciousness and rarely reveals her true feelings—even with people she has worked with for 15 years.

Comparing the two is enlightening. Maria pushes past her limits while Ms. M. hides behind them. Both are self-conscious, but Maria is taking chances, becoming involved and not so afraid of negative consequences.

Over-Dependence

Highly bloated upper loops

Exaggerated roundedness

Lower loops pulling leftwards

Narrow letters—cramped words

Cradled or X-shaped "I"

Downward, light pressure t-bar

Concave connecting strokes proceeding directly from one letter to the next without returning to the baseline

Any of the characteristics shown above, as well as Pleaser and Re-actor slants, indicate a person's need for approval in order to feel all right. If you see these traits in peoples' handwriting, give them plenty of reassurance, and you'll make their lives easier. Some people can't seem to get enough love, admiration and attention. Pleasers and Reactors handle this type of dependence in others very well because they need to feel needed. (Whether that's desirable or not is another question.)

If you run into all the characteristics shown above in one person's writing, try to get the writer to go for some kind of help.

Depression

do much and

Handwriting that droops at line or word endings shows a depressed state of mind. If it's chronic, it may be biological and/or hereditary.

Irrational Pride

tall t's tell a lot

Tall, narrow capitals reflect standoffishness and vanity. So do t-stems times at least two and a half times higher than lower case letters. These writers won't reveal what they're feeling, because they think that if they do, they'll be too vulnerable. This may be from fear of ridicule, or because they believe it's none of your business.

Most rightward slanters, Chameleons and those who don't leave space between words feel threatened when they're around people with this kind of aloofness. Thinkers and Menders handle it just fine.

Resentment

resentment strokes

"In 1943 your Aunt Mildred manipulated your grandmother into leaving her all the family jewels. That's why you can't give Susan a decent engagement ring."

Holding tightly to the past, resentful people can create the impression that ancient misdeeds happened just yesterday.

The origin of the word resentment tells the whole story. Resentment derives from the latin word *sentire*, which means "to feel." The prefix "re" means again. Therefore resentment means to feel again—and again—and again. Resentment means never having to say, "Let bygones be bygones."

Resentment strokes are introductory lines that look like braces or knife blades rising from below the baseline. These strokes don't bend. They're always straight and rigid.

Miserliness

I'm noticing that

Has anyone ever handed you a ten dollar bill in such a way that you felt a tug of resistance—as though the person was reluctant to release it? You were probably accepting a "gift" from a person who spaces letters within words very tightly. This isn't a deadly trait, but it may irritate those who write with long, swinging, generous word endings.

Don't confuse frugality with stinginess. Frugal writers end words abruptly—omitting any finishing strokes. This is a positive trait, because it indicates that the writers are self-sufficient and not dependent on anyone else's approval.

Caution

Caution

Caution appears in handwriting like the skid marks of a car trying to avoid a collision. If chronic, these writers may vacillate so long before taking action that they miss the boat. Caution is a red light when it becomes fearfulnesss and makes the person reluctant to make commitments.

Feeling Victimized

demonstrate

You're on a plane seated next to a little old lady. Within twenty minutes you know all about how her children and grandchildren take advantage of her. You listen to the gory details of her late husband's prostate cancer and then how the government took her life savings during probate. And before you can tear into your vacuum-packed peanuts, she tells you how her sister choked to death on those same peanuts.

You've just met a professional victim. Ten to one this person's writing will reveal shallow, concave t-bars and endings that sweep over to the left. There may be passive aggressive garlands, too!

Irritability and Temper

Jagged and angular

Slashed right i-dots

Right-of-the-stem t-bars

Barbs leading into first
letters of words—usually
on capital m's

"I's" with two tails pointing to the right

All these signals can alert you to professional finger-pointers and
irritable blamers. If you find any of these configurations in your
friends' writing, now you know that it's their disposition and not
you that is causing the problems. If this is your handwriting, you
might lighten up by not expecting so much of yourself and others.

Temper Tantrums

Long and sharply pointed endings reveal people who make it almost
impossible for you to relate to them on a deep level. Sarcasm is
high on their agenda. You need to be a Thinker not to take it
personally.

Defensiveness & Over-Sensitivity to Criticism

As mentioned before, loops don't belong in the "t" or "d." Looped
"d's" mean sensitivity to criticism and defensiveness about personal

habits. Looped "t's" mean sensitivity about work performance. So be careful about telling looped d'ers and t'ers to do things your way. At best, you'll hurt their feelings. At worst, you'll raise a defensive storm.

Manipulation

| Thread | Large writing | Arcade endings |

Did you ever lend money to a friend so he could pay his rent only to find out he spent your money on a vacation? Or have you sworn to the teacher that your child wouldn't skip school—only to learn he actually did it? At one time or another, we've all been manipulated. Children and alcoholics are among the most talented manipulators, but there are many others. Look for faint threads or large writing. Thready, wispy strokes and arcade endings indicate secret motives and a person who may be concealing something.

Argumentativeness

Black belts in verbal abuse make "p's" with very high extensions into the upper zone. You cannot make looped "d's" or "t's" and get along with them!

Jealousy

| Jagged writing | Teeny loops introducing letters (usually upper case) |

Reactor slant

If people are jealous, it usually means they don't feel lovable. And it's hard to convince them they are, because they're always looking for evidence that they aren't. If the personal pronoun "I" has a tiny loop, jealousy is a chronic and crucial part of this writer's life.

Aggressiveness (not to be confused with assertiveness) & Hostility

Angular lower loops

Jagged writing

Stabs in middle or lower zones and stabs at the baseline indicate people who believe the world is a hostile place, so they're going to be hostile right back!

If you make looped "d's" and "t's" and are a Pleaser or Reactor, you'll have a difficult time getting along with aggressive people. You'll tend to take their abruptness and slurs personally. But if you have to work with or under such folk, keep in mind that it's their problem and not yours, unless you choose to make it yours. The best way to deal with it may be to keep your distance.

Sadism

Blunt, clublike endings in the middle zone indicate sadistic tendencies. Blunt endings below the line show brutality. The ink seems to pool at the ends.

Mass murderer Richard Speck, convicted assassin of Robert Kennedy Sirhan Sirhan, and David "Son of Sam" Berkowitz all had this handwriting trait.

Violence

Any of the following signals should make you suspicious. But if the writing you examine has more than three of these violent traits, beware.

Muddy

Misplaced pressure is heavy upstroke pressure and light downstroke pressure.

Heavy, downward t-bars

Club endings: "t's," lower zone

Downward endings

Sharp downward, vertical endings

Sharp daggers in lower zone

Slash strokes and horizontal pressure

Very heavy pressure

Angular lower non-loops

Maniac letters

Clubbed "d"

Written over letters

Jump-up letters in middle zone

Inky ovals

Pointed loops

Weird arcades

Extreme angles

Pathological Lying

Huge capitals

High and left t-bars or above-the-stem t-bars

Erratic or flattened middle zone

Very tall and loopy upper zone letters

Very light pressure on upstrokes and rightward strokes

Remember, most of these writing traits are all right if they don't appear along with the others in this section. But, again, if more than three of these traits show up, beware.

22. The Handwriting Analysis Dishonesty Checklist

"But he didn't tell me he was married!"

"I promise, if I'm elected, that I won't raise taxes."

"I never even went near your car, mom. Honest. You don't think I put that scrape in it!"

"I don't smell cigarette smoke, dad. You must be hallucinating."

Sound familiar? These lies range from white to not so white, but they are all lies, nonetheless. There's no promise you won't fall for shady deals ever again, but this chapter will give you some great tools for judging a person's reliability.

Don't forget, however, that there are different types of dishonesty. Honesty is an ambiguous word. For example, if you say you're a Robert Redford look-alike, when you actually resemble Arnold Stang, you may be dishonest or simply "self-delusional."

Or if scatterbrains omit crucial information in the rush to complete a report, are they guilty of deceit, "lying by omission," or just carelessness?

Dozens of handwriting factors are involved in dishonesty. But in this chapter we'll be looking at the fourteen major ones. Most writing contains at least one or two of them. If you find any example that's 100% pure, you've found a rare bird. But—and this is important—before you decide people are dishonest on the basis of their handwriting, make sure they have *four or more* of the characteristics listed.

Left Loops on Ovals

Left loopers tell lies to *themselves,* and defend their erroneous attitudes, beliefs and actions so that they can avoid painful realizations about themselves and others. They say things like, "I should introduce sister Grace to my business partner (even though I know they'd hate each other), because dad told me she's lonely these days."

This self-deception harms the writer and usually irritates friends and spouses—but it never disturbs the parents of the looper. After all, many parents think their kids should feel guilty. And these writers have plenty of guilty feelings or they wouldn't left-loop their ovals.

Overly-generous, eternally nice, perennial do-gooders often left-loop their vowels. They feel guilty when they don't help others, and resentful when they do help and aren't appreciated.

Left-looping also occurs when people resist major changes. It may appear at the end of a relationship when you pretend you don't care, or when you get the golden handshake from the firm you've been with for twenty years. When left-loopers stop pretending big things are minor inconveniences, they gradually stop writing with left loops.

Right Loops

doing computerized

By themselves, right-sided oval loops tell us the writer is concealing feelings and facts. Huge right loops indicate chronic beat-around-the-bushism disease. It's as common as colds, but the only known cure for the right-looper is to speak frankly and without reservation or fear of recrimination. It helps too if the writer doesn't try to keep secrets.

Both Loops

lack of sexual

Extraordinarily loopy witers are professionally indirect. They can usually master sensitivity training language to the point of madness.

"I feel that you are not acknowledging my communication, but I hear where you're coming from."

These right and left loopers are covering up feelings of inadequacy and they're doing a great job. You'd have to be an FBI agent to know what they're really thinking and feeling. You might not feel sure whether they're telling the truth.

Illegible Writing

Illegible writers don't want their behind-the-scenes activities known. Recall President Nixon's Watergate signature? A total scrawl. Generally, illegibility indicates manipulation and hidden motives.

Gapped Bottoms

Gapped bottoms are extremely rare. Graphologists call them "Embezzlers' Ovals." These "breaks" at the baseline are a blatant indication of dishonesty. I've only seen them in forgers' handwriting. Keep track of your wallet, your jewelry and your bank book when you find them.

Jerky Writing

Jerky writing looks as though a right-hander used the left hand to write with. Don't confuse this with the writing of someone who has arthritic hands or has had a stroke.

Jerky writers change directions often and are generally Chameleons, too. And you know that Chameleons are undependable and unpredictable, so you know what to expect.

Backtracking

conversation, circles amnesty

Notice that going back and writing over a mistake makes a bigger mess than simply crossing it out and writing above the error. Backtrackers try to cover mistakes in their handwriting (and their lives) in hopes no one will notice. But guess what? It's very obvious when you're trying to hide something.

"I don't know anything about that India ink spill on the new carpet. The dog must have done it."

"Did the dog try to clean it up, too? And who else uses India ink around here?"

Backtrackers usually mess things badly in the cover-up process, which might indicate that they unconsciously want to be caught. Forgers are notorious for this handwriting trait.

Two-Faced Writing

I think you should

Two introductory strokes on more than a few words, (at least six on a page) means the writer is wearing a deceptive facade. Like double t-bars, this characteristic is rare.

Unreadable Signature

Signatures can be radically different from the rest of the writing. Doctors, lawyers and people who have to sign their names many times each day often simplify their signatures. In other cases, the writers enjoy secrecy or prefer to keep their private thoughts private. If the rest of the writing is sloppy, you're probably dealing with a person who is inconsistent.

Obiously Msing Letrs

attactive

When letters are obviously missing from words, you can be sure the writer is impulsive and doesn't take all available information into account. By itself this kind of dishonesty isn't harmful, but with three other dishonesty factors, the person will lie by omission.

Elaborate Writing

elaborate

Extreme vanity is the keynote of the frilly writer. We have already looked at the tremendously tall "t's" that may be a feature of this trait. Why is elaborate writing a sign of dishonesty? To the elaborate writer, the plain truth is dull, and the greatest sin is to be boring. So the fancy writer puts on airs and false fronts to make an impression. The plain truth is that the simpler the writing, the more captivating the writer.

Complicated Writing

Hank   *Dorcey*

"I'm sorry I'm late, but I couldn't find my car keys, and then the cat wouldn't get out from under the car, and then I had to stop for gas, but I didn't have my credit card, and I had to use cash. So then I had to go to the bank, but the teller said I was overdrawn. So I had to go downtown and get some money from Jack because I didn't want to borrow the money from you, and then I . . . ."

Complicated writing suggests a life so dull, the writers need to make things appear to be more interesting and involved than they are. These writers invent extraneous details. This trait is associated with dishonesty because often the complications are exaggerated or fictional and generally sensational.

Undulating Writing

*mone and experience my desire now in
I've spent most of the time very immor*

Undulators disregard the baseline. Baselines represent reality. Following this logic, undulators have a disregard for reality, and this means *your* reality. So in many cases you can't depend upon them to follow through, to tell a story straight or to keep promises. Undulation also symbolizes drastic mood swings and "flexible" moral values.

DifFerEnt Ways of Writing the Same LeTter

self-satisfied

ArE caPital letters insErtEd where thEy don'T belOng? Is one letter wriTten in script in some pLaces and not in oTherS? This is another cover-up signal and indicates rebelliousness. Inconsistent writing means inconsistent behavior. This isn't an alarming habit; most people practice it, and a certain degree of defiance is the "American Way." But if three other dishonesty factors appear, this rebelliousness may be a rationalization for the writer's dishonesty.

That is the 14 point dishonesty checklist. Again, please don't judge handwriting as dishonest without seeing at least FOUR of these factors. And keep in mind that double loops, illegibility, gapped bottoms and jerky writing are the most important of these indicators.

23. The Compatibility Test

The Compatibility Test will show you how to figure out the potential of any relationship.

Before you take the test, read about your slant in relation to the other person's slant in Part 2. Then go on to read the paragraphs that relate to the two of you in the section on Compatibilities of Letter Shapes and Connections in Part 3.

Finally, to take the test, sit down with both samples of handwriting and a blank sheet of paper with your name and the other person's name at the top. Follow the instructions and keep a running tabulation of your compatibility score as you go.

1. Determine the person's slant:
   - If the slant is the same as yours, score 60 points.
   - If it's the slant next to yours, score 40 points.
   - If the slant is two away from yours, score 20 points.
   - If it's more than two slants away, score 10 points.
2. Is the basic handwriting shape Garlander, Rounder, Arcade, Angular or Thready? (see pages 96-110)
   - If it matches yours, score 50 points.
   - If you like that shape style's description, score 40 points.
   - If you're an Arcader, Garlander or Angular, score 10 for Thready.
   - If after reading that shape's description, you feel you couldn't relate, score 0 points.
3. What type of communication vowels does the writing have? (see pages 136-141)
   - If the oval letters match yours, score 50 points.
   - If the oval letters aren't the same as yours, but you think you could communicate clearly with that person, score 40 points.
   - If the oval letters are any other type, score 20 points.
   - If the handwriting has explosive vowels, score 0.

4. Which zone is emphasized, upper, middle or lower? Or is the writing balanced in all three zones?
   - If it's the same as yours, score 50 points.
   - If it's close in appearance, score 40 points.
   - If it's totally opposite to your own, score 10 points.
5. What is the spacing type: crowded, loose or balanced? (see pages 141-150)
   - If the spacing matches yours, score 50 points.
   - If it's balanced, and yours isn't, score 40 points.
   - If it's crowded and yours is loose, score 0 points.
   - If it's loose and yours is crowded, score 0 points.
6. Is it sharp, rounded or compressed? (see pages 128-129)
   - If the thinking style matches yours, score 50 points.
   - If after reading about the thinking style which is different from your own, you decide to take a chance, score 40 points.
   - If you don't think you could relate, score 0 points.
7. Is the writing connected, partially connected or disconnected?
   - If it's the same as yours, score 40 points.
   - If your writing is totally connected or totally disconnected and the other person's writing is partially connected, score 25 points.
   - If your writing is totally connected and the other writing is totally disconnected, score 0 points.
   - If your writing is totally disconnected and the other writing is totally connected, score 0 points.
8. What kind of lower loops does the writer make most often?
   - If they match yours score 35.
   - If they're close, score 30.
   - If they drop down to encompass more than one line below or if they don't exist at all, score 15.
   - If they are highly angular, score 0.
9. What is the writer's energy level? (see pages 161-163).
   - If it matches your own, score 20 points.
   - If it's almost the same, score 10.
   - If one writer is extremely light, while the other is extremely heavy, score 0.
10. Give 10 points for each Green Light (Chapter 20).

11. Deduct 10 points for each Red Light (Chapter 21).

12. Deduct 5 points for each dishonesty trait you find in the handwriting, but deduct 50 points each for consistent double looping, total illegibility and gapped bottoms.

Add up the score. If you scored from 450 to 650, you've found a rare relationship, perhaps even a soul mate.

If you scored 280 to 445, you have differences to work out, but it's a good match.

In the -70 to 275 range, your differences won't be easy to reconcile. If you tend to put yourself down for making bad choices, and friends gloat when they say "I told you so," you might consider letting this relationship go. If the person is aggressive (using Atilla lower loops with angular writing, for example), be very careful. Also, if there are more than four Red Lights, it might be a good idea to keep your distance.

If you scored lower than -70, look out. You can't change a tiger into a kitten, but you can learn to live with either one—if you want to and if you aren't allergic to cats. You've got to do a lot to make this relationship work. Ask yourself if you need another full-time job and proceed with caution.

If you scored low in a relationship that you can't walk away from, such as parent-child, student-teacher or on-the-job, look for drastic differences in your handwriting samples. The differences will be obvious and big. For instance, your writing may be very small compared to the other, or yours may be round while the other is all angles, or you may leave wide spaces between letters and the other person doesn't.

Once you identify the basic handwriting differences, turn to the chapter that discusses those differences. Maybe reading about them in a graphological light will ease the tension in the relationship. But at least it will help you to understand that your problems are no one's fault. They are only differences, after all. Perhaps by realizing that, you'll be able to deal with each other in a more loving way.

Part 5
The Letters—A to Z

24. Upper Case Letters

A B C D E F G H I J K L

Printed upper case letters: A refined, aesthetic sense; freedom from following the crowd; intelligence and love of literature.

Apple Banana Cola Dimple

Printed capitals with cursive: An appreciation for life's simple pleasures, such as clean sheets, white shirts and spring flowers in a Mason jar.

a B C D E G H I J L

Palmer-style upper-case letters: Conservative, practical point of view influences thinking about politics, clothing style and basic, established values.

A B C D E F H

Narrow upper case letters: Shy, reserved nature; pride.

A B C R

Deliberate downstrokes leading into capital letters: Inspiration from "above." Makes use of a natural meditative process and is notably perceptive.

Low bars on A, H and K: Low goals directly related to lack of achievement in the past. Needs to develop a more optimistic attitude and elevate aspirations.

Knotted bars on A, H and K: Persistent nature.

Complicated upper case letters: Extravagant tastes. Wants to be known as having upper class refinement.

Wide open A, O and D: Feels an urgency to talk constantly and not likely to follow through on the ideas generated. Uncomfortable with silence and may be a chronic interrupter.

Bloated top halves of B and R: Easily swayed by others' opinions. An indication of rebelliousness.

Sharp angular jabs at the baseline in upper and lower case letters: Demands (doesn't request) perfection from self and others.

Claw capital T and F: Hostility. Carries over anger from the past. Often believes these feelings have been dealt with successfully, but they haven't. Forgiveness is needed.

Broad sweeps to the left in any zone: Guilt feelings.

Separated sections in the D, K and R: A reluctance to get intimately involved with others. These writers feel they have enough problems of their own to cope with and don't need to be involved with anyone else's.

Little loops or tiny hooks on the beginning of upper and lower case letters: Jealousy and the fear that the writer doesn't deserve to be loved.

A and O: little openings: Modesty.

B FORMATIONS

Wide Bottom: Gullibility. If these writers get into trouble in relationships, it's because they believe anything they're told. Could greatly benefit from studying graphology, which will help them to be more discriminating.

Wide left side: Wears a false front. Few people really know what lies beneath that facade.

C FORMATIONS

C begins with a downstroke: Inspirational thinking. These writers seem to know things without knowing how they know. This is an unconscious (as opposed to psychic process).

Semi-box C: Enjoys working with the hands; manual dexterity.

Squiggles within the C: A tendency to make things more complicated than they need to be.

Angular C: A clever, quick-thinking person.

D FORMATIONS

Left-directional base: Feelings of self-importance, which may be or may not be justified.

Closed top: Secretive and discreet.

Wavy ending: Flirtatious.

Wide: Self-centered; fascinated with self and own accomplishments.

Pointed top: Intellectual mentality.

E FORMATIONS

Upper Looped: Vanity

Angular: Intelligent, but needs to develop more flexibility so others can understand their genius.

F FORMATIONS

Big hook: Collector of money, seashells, antiques.

Long overstroke extending to the right: A paternal and protective person.

G FORMATIONS

Figure Eight: Glib and verbally versatile. An indication of creative writing ability.

Loopy and Knotted: Cluttered thinking; needs to spend less time on nonessentials.

H FORMATIONS

Created in one elaborate stroke: Enjoys solving elaborate problems and puzzles (crossword, mazes, mysteries).

I FORMATIONS

Connected at top and bottom of printed I: Feelings of independence.

Disconnected at top of printed I: Father ruled childhood home.

Disconnected at bottom of printed I: Mother ruled childhood home.

Overly large vertical loop to form the I: A need to cut mother's apron strings. These writers are also too attached to their own opinions.

No vertical loop with a large horizontal loop: Needs to develop self-reliance instead of trying to please dear old Dad.

Small and curled up I: Feelings of inferiority.

Large I: These writers like to think they're better than everyone else to cover up a shaky ego.

Left-leaning I: Overly self-critical.

Right-leaning I: Overly critical of others

Backwards (begins at arrow): Hidden hostility and resentment towards people who offer advice.

Appears like a "d": Overly sensitive and defensive.

Appears like a fetus: Needs affection.

Small i used as upper case I: Doesn't give self enough credit for jobs well done.

I as a dollar sign: Money-conscious. Parents represent wealth to the writer.

Angular: Overly critical when dealing with other people. These writers should remember Grandma's adage: You catch more flies with honey than with vinegar!

Sticklike: Easily bruised ego.

J FORMATION

Note: Many "J's" can be analyzed by looking at the "I" section, since both letters are traditionally formed with two loops.

Pointed top: Penetrating mind.

K FORMATIONS

Tall upper right stroke: Ambitious in a positive way.

Printed: A no-nonsense person—very straightforward.

Both sections connected with a knot: Loves to be caressed; affectionate.

L FORMATIONS

No lower loop: Aloof.

Huge left, lower loop: A sign of egotism.

Big upper loop: Enjoys taking care of others.

Hook: Avaricious.

M & N FORMATIONS

Curved lead-in: Sense of humor—developed to overcome life's rough spots.

Straight, little lead-in: Bad temper.

Loop enclosed and connected to main part of M: Secretive.

Straight vertical lines (2 for N, 3 for M) with a "roof": Sense of beauty and natural intelligence.

Introductory loop: Desire for responsibility.

Open-ended loop: Desire for responsibility, but unable to handle it once it has been obtained.

Left hump higher than right hump: Values own opinion over others' and may be tactless.

Right hump higher than left hump: Self-consciousness comes from underrating own opinions. Unlikely to reveal true feelings out of fear they won't be taken seriously.

Middle stroke doesn't reach baseline: Dreams seem unattainable, because writer isn't going all out to make them come true. These writers try to accomplish goals the easy way.

Hooked lead-in: One of the indications of dishonesty. These writers hide information "behind their backs."

Looped in three places: A worrier.

P FORMATIONS

Balloonlike: A dreamer with a high opinion of self.

Ends left of stem: Known for having good judgment.

S FORMATIONS

Looks like a treble clef: Musical ability or great appreciation of music.

Ends at left: These writers feel others should be as self-reliant as they are.

Big and rounded: Relaxed and easy-going.

T FORMATIONS

Printed with bar extending more right than left: Protective of others.

Wavy, high bar: Flashy dresser.

V FORMATIONS

Higher right than left side: Rebellious and hates being told what to do; enterprising.

High, horizontal and angular: Protective of others; likely to defend loved ones with a vengeance.

W FORMATIONS

Angular: Ready for action.

Rounded: Passivity towards attaining goals; preoccupation with buns—not the kind at McDonalds.

X FORMATIONS

Blunt ending: Hostility; easily angered.

High, upper right extension: Enterprising and ambitious nature.

Z FORMATION

Long, lower right extension: Pride in achievements.

25. Lower Case Letters

A & O FORMATIONS

 *Wide open:* Talkative.

 *Closed:* Secretive and trustworthy.

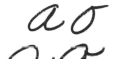 *Large left, inner loop:* Self-deceptive.

 *Loop on right:* Secretive.

 *Long lead-ins:* Doesn't like dealing with details, but loves handling big problems.

 *Double loops:* Hides true feelings from self and others.

 No lead-in: Direct communications and usually rapid thinking.

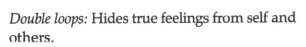 *Little inner circles:* These writers think they're being discreet, but actually they tell little white lies.

 *Covered-over:* Protective of self.

Inner hooks: An indication of deceitfulness.

Open bottoms: An indication of dishonesty. The "Embezzler Oval."

B FORMATIONS

Open lip: Gullibility.

Closed lip: Skepticism.

Big loop: Likes compliments.

Lead-in from above: Strict religious upbringing.

D FORMATIONS

Short stem: Indpendent thinking and possible defensiveness about life-style and ideas.

Tall stem: Proud, restrained and formal.

Wavy top: A love 'em and leave 'em attitude.

Looped over stem: Slow and deliberate.

No loop: Terrific listener.

Looped: Sensitive and defensive when it comes to criticism of personal habits.

Lots of loops: Another indication of dishonesty.

Looks like musical "flat": Musical bent.

Starts from the top and goes down: Overly idealistic.

E FORMATIONS

Enclosed: Closed-minded.

Open: Open to new solutions and ideas.

Narrow loop: Places too much importance on being right.

Greek e: Loves classical art forms.

Long ending: Needs to be in the spotlight, the center of attention.

Filled with extra ink: Hypersensitive and hypersexual.

F FORMATIONS

Even loops: Well organized.

Large lower loops with no upper loops: Many urges (exercise, sex, eating and making money); active and energetic; needs to plan before acting.

Big, puffy loops: Possible eating disorder; obesity.

Large upper loop with no lower loop: Prefers mental to physical activities; likes to work with tools close by so it's not necessary to get out of the chair.

Figure eight: Natural verbal ability; excels at self-expression.

With opening at baseline: Confidence.

No opening at baseline: Doesn't often consider the opinions of others.

Pointed tops and bottoms: Independent and self-reliant.

Angular: Artistic flair, loves being surrounded with beautiful objects.

Looks like a Christian cross: Self-righteous; feels like a martyr.

Ink inside lower loop: Self-indulgence.

G FORMATIONS—
Lower Loops

Tiny, lower loop: Exclusive in choosing friends.

Very full loop: Needs many friends, activities, choices and general variety; an indication of extreme restlessness.

Figure eight: Creative writing or speaking ability.

Open-ended: Sexually and socially unfulfilled. Finances, or lack of them, are of great concern.

Angular or triangulated: Unusual sexual and/or monetary desires.

Left-roving: Guilt feelings.

Abrupt ascension to the right: Aggressive in almost every area; likely to have many strong opinions.

Ending in a droop: Sad feelings about social, sexual or financial situation.

Ending high above the baseline: Optimistic about social, sexual and financial situation.

Open bottoms: Doesn't consider all possibilities before making social and financial choices.

No loop: Avoids intimacy; feels awkward when faced with affection.

Modestly full loop finishing at the baseline: Adept in the social graces; wants to be close and communicative with friends.

H FORMATIONS

Ending below the baseline: Pessimistic; fatigued; possibly chronic depression.

Upper extension very short: Preoccupied with daily activities at the expense of developing imagination.

Narrow high loops: Strict religious training.

No space between arch and initial stroke: Repression of talents, thoughts and actions. These writers aren't doing what they really want to do with their lives.

Large gap between arch and initial stroke: Full expression of talents, thoughts and actions.

K FORMATIONS

Rounded: Broadminded.

Ballooned: Rebellious.

Fancy construction: Pride in appearance.

Wide and simple: Not particularly interested in outward appearances.

L FORMATIONS

Sharp top: Sharp mind. These writers believe they know things no one else knows.

Huge loops: Highly imaginative.

Narrow loops: Narrow minded; limited imagination; a good researcher.

Sticklike: Simple and intuitive thinking process.

Second l taller than the first: Self-consciousness. These writers believe other people will pounce on their mistakes.

M & N FORMATIONS

Well-shaped: Natural student and quick thinker.

Rounded: Creative thinking.

Sharp tops: Investigative mind.

Retraced inside the letter: Creativity is kept on hold.

Caved-in on right side: Insecure because of a lack of affection in infancy and early childhood. These writers tend to project an unloving mother image onto authority figures throughout their lives unless they come to terms with their unfulfilled needs for affection. Often they don't know what to do with affection once they find a loving mate. They're also concerned with their physical appearance and have difficulty accepting the way they look.

These writers often feel pressured about the future, and when faced with urgent problems, ask for advice instead of drawing upon their own resources. If they can learn to accept affection, however slowly, and give a bit more, allowing themselves to feel deeply, these problems may be alleviated.

Four humps: Apt to be accident prone.

Tiny loops at the tops: An indication of clairvoyance.

Loops created on upstrokes: Overly concerned about others.

Loop on introductory stroke: These writers pretend they aren't worrying, but they are.

Short, aborted ending: One of the indications of dishonesty and a sign of ambition.

"Spiked": Enormous pride in self.

Hooks: Avaricious.

Wavy introductory stroke: Sense of humor.

P FORMATIONS

Large left-sided bubble: Need for, and love of, exercise.

Bowl-like structure at baseline: Likes being taken care of.

High "spike" reaching into the upper zone: Argumentative; not shy about expressing opinions.

Open at baseline: Relaxed and carefree.

Closed at baseline: Thrifty, economical.

Tiny loop at beginning: Imaginative.

Retraced downstroke: repression of basic urges; a dislike of exercise.

R FORMATIONS

Flat top: mechanical ability.

Sharp tentlike structure: Sharp mind.

Rounded top: Lack of intellectual curiosity.

Greek E: Great fondness for literature and reading.

Printed capital R in regular cursive writing: Rebellious.

Looped top: Overly worried; love of singing.

S FORMATIONS

Pointed: Stubborn; lives by own values.

Rounded: Yielding; easily influenced by friends.

Ends at left: Self-reliance.

Hooked over: Avaricious.

Looped: Tenacity.

Printed s while rest of writing is cursive: Appreciation of beauty. These writers would rather have no furniture than ugly furniture.

Dish shape for the s to rest on: Wants to be taken care of.

T FORMATIONS

Looped stem: Sensitive to criticism of work.

Tent-shaped: Stubborn.

T at least three times taller than rest of lower case letters: Pride and vanity.

Short: Indepedent thinking.

Looped-over: Laziness.

Light bar: Can't handle competition; will-power needs a boost.

Medium darkened bar: Willpower fades quickly; needs to plan more before taking action.

Heavy bar: Forceful willpower.

Above the stem: Idealistic dreamer.

Bar halfway up the stem: Realistic and reachable goals.

Low bar: Low goals.

Bar underneath the stem: Disappointed by past failures.

Very long bar: Driven towards success. These writers believe everyone else shares that drive. They can be difficult to work with.

Wavy, long bar: High enthusiasm and optimism.

Short bar: Underachiever.

Convex bar: An attempt is being made to control faults.

Concave bar: Naive.

Bar to the left of stem: Procrastination.

Bar to the right of stem: Impatient and easily irritated.

Star-shaped: Good common sense.

Knot at left: Persistent and economical.

Ends at left: Concerned about self and perhaps egotistical.

No bar: Absentminded.

Downward bar: Controlling and domineering.

Sharp end: Apt to control and dominate others with sarcasm.

Blunt end on bar: Hostility.

Wavy bar: Not serious about career and goals.

Ending to the right without crossing: Sensitive; well developed sense of smell and taste. People who were born in the 1920's through the 1940's were taught to make final t's this way.

Drooping version of the one before this one: Pessimistic.

Hooks on bar: Tenacious.

Different ways of making the t and bar: Need for goal clarification; versatiltiy.

U FORMATION

Angular at baseline: Economical with time.

V FORMATIONS

Cover stroke: Protective.

W FORMATIONS

Wavy introductory stroke: Sense of humor gets this person through the day.

Straight, short introductory stroke: Temperamental.

Angular at baseline: Active and ready for anything.

Loop at end: Has a soft and gentle touch.

Ending sweeps to the left: Cautious and fearful about the future.

Rounded bottom: Feels the need to gather more information before proceeding. This is an indication of being stuck in a routine.

AFTERWORD

Some graphologists say that the key to interpreting handwriting is in the connections (garlands, arcades, etc.). Others say that it's best to analyze it through intricate calculations entered on a wheel called a Psychogram. There is also a mail-order school that teaches handwriting analysis trait by trait, and it calls its graduates "Graphoanalysts."

Whatever system you follow, your goal is to see handwriting as a portrait of the personality. You'll know you're on the right track if you can determine more about people from their handwriting than you could from actually becoming acquainted with them. You've already learned the elements of handwriting in this book. If you want to get started analyzing the handwriting of friends and relatives, you're ready to begin. Do it as much as you can. Get lots of practice. Every time you see a few lines of writing, think about what you already know from the slant, the letter formations and the spacing. You will know a great deal. But remember that if you want to truly capture the essence of someone's personality, you'll need to develop and trust your intuition. That's always working— whether you're aware of it or not.

Please don't be afraid to make mistakes. It's tempting to be the "expert," but questions are sure to arise that you won't know the answers to. You'll feel on the spot. But remember that you really aren't. When you're stumped, just say you're still learning, and you'll get back to them when you find the answer. Or you could say, "Now that curlicue looks interesting. I wonder what that means." Or you might guess at the meaning by saying, for example, "Most books claim that tall 't's' indicate a lot of pride. Do you think that's true of you?" Then if your subjects don't have double-looped vowels (or a few of the other dishonesty traits on pages 190-195), you'll probably be able to believe what they tell you.

If you decide you want to do advanced work in graphology, find a teacher who will encourage you to assess handwriting as a whole picture. If you can't find any graphologists listed in your yellow pages, and/or you really want to learn more than the basics presented in this book, write to my professional society: the American Handwriting Analysis Foundation, P.O. Box 6201, San Jose, CA 95101. Or write Marjorie Westergaard at 411 Lakewood Circle, A907, Colorado Springs, CO 80910 for information about her annual *Director of Handwriting Analysts*, which lists the graphologists who are also teachers.

Graphology is my career. I use it, along with my background in business and industrial psychology, to help many Southern California companies select personnel more effectively. My clients range from aerospace corporations to book publishers and from medical and realty offices to print shops. I also write a column on graphology in personnel selection and other workplace issues.

In the community I apply handwriting analysis to career guidance programs, team counselling with chemically dependent clients and patients, and to help new business owners find their strengths and weaknesses.

I've also been teaching graphology for quite a few years and, if you haven't guessed, I am particularly interested in new applications, methods and procedures. That's why I created the Los Angeles Handwriting Analysis Society with graphologists Steve Borisoff and Abe Lansberg. We conduct research in many areas. Currently we're investigating the handwriting of co-dependents (mages and other family members of alcoholics). So far our findings parallel Robin Norwood's in her book *Women Who Love Too Much*: The handwriting of co-dependents seem to have more in common than the handwriting of alcoholics does!

I encourage you to keep studying and practicing. Read all the books you can get your hands on. I think Amend and Ruiz' *Handwriting Analysis: The Complete Basic Book* (Newcastle, 1980) is an excellent book for intermediate as well as advanced students, and there are many other good ones.

Graphology has been an exciting and rewarding path for me. If you're considering making it your career, know that it takes many, many years to get a steady practice going, and business knowledge is essential. In order to call yourself a graphologist, you should be a certified member of one of the societies within the Council of Graphological Societies. And it's my personal belief that you should also have been using graphology on a daily basis for at least seven years before you set out to do it professionally.

The best thing about graphology? It has enabled me to understand myself and the other people in my life far better than I ever could without it. I've become less critical and more accepting of myself, my friends and my family—especially my family. It's a lot easier for me now to accept them as they are, rather than keep trying to change them. I hope that, as you use this book, it will bring you closer to your own true nature, your strengths and your potential—and that it will bring you closer to others as well.

Index